THE BONDI BUBBLE

MEGAN KROLIK

To Lee, the first person to truly believe I could do this. Thanks for all the beers and beta reads and Bondi adventures!

And to Emmi, Elissa and Aurora, my favourite bookworms. Your parents said you probably shouldn't read this until you are 18 but I promise I'll sneak you a copy if you promise not to tell them!

ONE

Dramorama *The Watson brothers are back in Byron with a very special+1...are wedding bells in the air for Rob and Tilly? #loveisintheair Click the link in our bio to find out all the juicy gossip from their loved-up trip down under!*

———

"Did that really, truly, really just happen?" asked Daisy in disbelief, as the posse of beautiful celebrities left her small boutique market stall in downtown Byron Bay.

Joe and Rob Watson, Hollywood mega-stars, brothers and Byron Bay locals had wandered into Daisy's stall an hour ago, along with Rob's American girlfriend, Grammy Award winner Tilly Bingham, some other familiar looking faces and a gaggle of cute kids and dogs. The celebrity group had then proceeded to buy up nearly all the contents of Garden and Bay, Daisy's small, eclectic fashion stall.

"This is that awesome organic place I got my pyjamas

from last time we were here," Tilly had said excitedly, before glancing over at Daisy in recognition.

"Hey, this was part of another market stall back then, right? You were selling a small range as part of another shop? You must be doing really well! Congratulations!" she said, beaming her megawatt Hollywood smile over at the dazed owner.

Tilly was right. Daisy was doing well. Well enough to employ a full-time staff member and expand into a profitable market stall and online store. Daisy's shop sold a range of t-shirts, tank tops, cotton pyjamas, scarves and accessories, all made with organic cotton sourced from local farms and traditional prints imported through an economic empowerment project run by Rise Beyond the Reef in Fiji. Daisy was proud that her shop was helping women in the South Pacific make an ethical living, while also supporting conservation and the traditional art of fabric printing that the women's communities were so famous for. It was something she wanted to do more of, if she ever got the chance.

"You're one of the Gardiners, right?" Tilly continued, chatting to Daisy as if they were old friends. "Our place is just down the road from you," she said, pulling out t-shirt after t-shirt and exclaiming at each one in delight.

"Do you mind if I Insta this?" she asked, holding up a shirt emblazoned with one of Daisy's own personal designs.

"Oh no, of course not," replied Daisy, frantically running around finding different sizes for her celebrity customers. In her haste, she tripped over her dog Elvis, who was busy making friends with everyone in the shop, and crashed into Tilly. Both of them tumbled onto the shop floor in a flurry of shirts, arms, and legs. Daisy was morti-fied, but Tilly collapsed into a fit of contagious giggles.

"I love this place! I love you! You look so adorable! Come here..."

Tilly pulled Daisy close and snapped a selfie of them laughing amongst a pile of shirts and scarves. Daisy's outfit of the day was an eclectic ensemble, even for her. Sleeping in on the busiest day of the week, plus a broken-down car meant she had thrown together the first things she found in her wardrobe - cutoff denim shorts, one of her singlets from the stall and a hand painted pink and blue silk robe which was technically meant for the bathroom. A flower crown she'd been experimenting with for the stall topped off the look. *Of all the days to be dressed like a boho hobo*, she laughed to herself ruefully. *But on the bright side, this is brilliant publicity, and I might be able to finally get my car fixed after these sales!*

"I'll share this to your socials," said Tilly. "Now that I've found you again, I'm going to replace all my tank tops. I've literally worn them all to death!"

Soon all the shopping and photographing was done, and the group started to leave. Tilly was the last to go, after hugging Daisy and Daisy's mum Lola tightly and giving Elvis one last scratch behind the ears.

Daisy took a deep breath, as the world slowly stopped spinning with gorgeous faces and bright, white teeth.

"Oh, weren't they lovely!" exclaimed Lola, turning slowly to survey the dishevelled stall. "Especially that red-haired boy, he was handsome! Do you think that was Prince Harry?"

"Oh mum," laughed Daisy, rolling her eyes affectionately at her mum. "As if Prince Harry would be hanging out in Byron!"

Daisy thought back to the red-haired man who had smiled so nicely at her and helped her up after her crash with Tilly. He looked familiar, and she felt like she had seen his face somewhere recently. Suddenly, she gasped in horror as she looked up at the speaker hanging on the tent pole in the corner of the shop. Was that Ed Sheeran, the famous English singer-songwriter? Had Ed Sheeran literally just been in her shop? She'd only been up to Brisbane to see his concert a few weeks ago, and she now had his latest album on high rotation in the shop. It couldn't have been him... could it?

Several hours later, as Daisy and her mum started to tidy up, the familiar ting of her tablet chirped in the background. It was a sound Daisy loved - it meant an online sale had come through. The first time she had heard it, she'd jumped up and down in excitement, and it still set off a small flurry of butterflies in her belly. To Daisy, it was the sound of success.

Ting. It went off again.

Then ting, ting, ting. Again and again and again.

Daisy and her mum looked at each other. What was going on?

Before they could investigate if the tablet was malfunctioning, a small hurricane in the form of a teenage girl rushed into the tent and threw her arms around Daisy.

"Daisy, you guys are all over social media! You met the Watsons! You met Tilly! Oh my goodness! This is the greatest day ever! What were they like? Tell me everything!"

Daisy extracted herself from the arms of her 17-year-old sister, Clementine, and reached for her mobile phone.

"What are you talking about, Clem? How did you know?"

"Daisy, look, your Instagram page has exploded! I was down at the beach with Zoe and Lara and suddenly there was a photo of you and Tilly everywhere!"

Daisy looked down at her phone in disbelief. Sure enough, there was the photo of Tilly and Daisy.

Oh no, thought Daisy in dismay. Tilly looked amazing, like a stylist had spent hours artfully posing her for a fashion shoot. Next to her, Daisy's long brown hair curled impetuously around her ears, her nose was still a touch red from her trip to the beach yesterday and the start of a pimple was emerging on her chin. Worse than that, her usually sparkly green eyes were crossed.

No wonder Tilly wanted to post it online, she thought, cringing with embarrassment. *Next to me, she looks amazing!*

Garden and Bay had a decent Instagram following, thanks mostly to the summer tourist trade and her stall at the annual winter music festivals. Clem helped her out on all things social and they had a small celebration recently, when they reached 10,000 followers.

But Daisy's stall now had nearly 15,000 followers on Instagram and over 5,000 likes on Facebook. Even her LinkedIn page was exploding with almost 500 new connection requests.

The tablet continued to ting merrily in the background. Lola slowly stepped behind the counter and opened up the online shop account. She flicked through a few orders before looking up at Daisy in disbelief.

Lola had recently been let go from her job at a local resort cleaning company, because of the post-Covid downturn. After getting bored with her unexpected 'funemployment', she had started helping Daisy at the stall on Saturday, her busiest day of the week. Despite her traditional Byron crystal and tie-dyed exterior, Lola was a savvy businesswoman. She knew her way around a business plan better than anyone in their small beach town and had quickly worked out the intricacies of the online ordering system.

"Umm, Daisy, I think you had better have a look at this," she said, her brow furrowed incredulously as she held out the tablet to her daughter.

A usual day saw maybe five to ten orders trickling in, with a few more overnight.

"Wow!" exclaimed Daisy, her eyes wide, as she took in the number of orders flooding in. There were over 150 unopened orders, and the number was steadily climbing.

Daisy's mobile started ringing. It was Heather from the local newspaper, Byron Shore News.

"Hey Daisy, is it true that Joe, Rob, and Tilly were at your stall today? Did you meet them? Can we get a quote for a story?"

"Oh, umm, hey Heather. Sorry things are a bit hectic here right now. Can I call you back later?"

"Ooh, they are still there, aren't they? Oh listen to me, you can't tell me that while they are standing there! Of course, I understand. I'll call you later...or you call me when they are out of the shop. Bye!"

Daisy ended the call with a wry laugh and looked over at her mum.

"That was the paper...oh mum, this is crazy! What is going on?"

Daisy's phone rang again.

"Hi there, is this the owner of Garden and Bay? My name is Erin, I'm calling from Oh-Em-G. Our editor Emma Green personally asked me to contact you for a comment about your meeting with Tilly Bingham this week. Is it true you are going into business together and opening a store in LA?"

"What? No, what? Where did you hear that? Sorry, I really can't talk right now. I'm so sorry..."

Daisy hung up the phone and stood in the middle of her stall, looking around at the rapidly increasing chaos. The small tent was now full of Clem and her friends, as well as curious neighbours and browsers, all piling in to ask questions and jostle for a spot to take their own selfies. Elvis was wild with joy at so many visitors and had designated himself the official welcoming committee, barking excitedly at each new arrival.

Daisy shivered. Suddenly everything felt very different, and she doubted her ordinary little life in Byron was ever going to be the same again.

———

A few days later, Garden and Bay's sales were still climbing, and the media interest hadn't let up.

Daisy arrived home with Lola after another busy market day and they both collapsed in relief around the kitchen table. Daisy's phone buzzed, and she wearily took it out of her pocket and scrolled through her messages. It was the third voicemail that made her sit up. Lola looked across at her daughter curiously, as Daisy's eyes widened with each passing minute.

"Mum, I think you should listen to this..."

Daisy put the phone on speaker and replayed the message.

"Hi Daisy, this is Saffron Williams from Thread Bare. I'm flying up to Byron this week and I would love to meet with you to see if you are interested in selling Garden and Bay. We think your brand would be an excellent fit for our company. Please call me back if you are interested in discussing our proposal further."

"What the heck is going on?" Daisy said, shaking her head in disbelief as she hung up the phone. "This week has been crazy!"

Lola looked at her eldest daughter pensively for a few moments before taking out her own phone and dialling a familiar number.

"Here darling," she said, passing the phone over to Daisy, who took it with a frown. "I know you are not going to like this, but there is one person you really need to speak to."

"Hello?" she said tentatively.

"Looks like you've hit the big time," drawled a familiar voice.

Daisy sighed in relief.

"Oh AB. Thank goodness. I think I need some help."

While most of Sydney knew Arabella McCarthy as the cool, calm and collected brains behind McCarthy PR, the city's top celebrity public relations firm, to Daisy, she was her sister-in-law and, once upon a time, best friend and partner in crime.

"I'm already packing...I'll be home in a few hours. In the meantime, stop answering the phone and talk to no one!"

Two

Byron Shore News *Music lovers were in for a treat this week when visiting rock star Ed Sheeran played a secret sunset show in the carpark by the pool. Beachgoers were treated to 40 minutes of acoustic singalongs, with superstar Tilly Bingham joining in for an energetic version of Men at Work's timeless classic 'Land Downunder'. For a full review and photos, head to www.byronshorenews.com.au*

———

Two whirlwind days later, Daisy and Arabella were sitting around the kitchen table at Daisy's family home. It was a well-worn, familiar place the two girls had sat in for many years, first as young kids, drawing or helping Daisy's dad bake cookies, then as teenagers, gossiping about friends, trying on makeup and secretly making plans to sneak out at night to meet boys.

But it had been a long time since the two friends had sat together like this.

Nowadays, Arabella and Daisy's brother Royce lived in an airy apartment overlooking Sydney's famous Bondi Beach. Arabella was running her successful PR firm and Royce worked as a photojournalist, covering national and international news stories for Associated Press. It was a career he had stumbled into after his stint fronting the band Mulligan's Mercy, an early 2000s Triple J Unearthed winner, famous for a time when they released their ARIA award winning album, Rockets and Rainbows.

Arabella's mum had died when she was in primary school, leaving behind a husband and a tribe of small children. Jeff McCarthy was a great father but overwhelmed with the responsibility of working full time and looking after three daughters. Living just one street away, Arabella and her sisters had become familiar faces around Lola and Bill's dinner table and the two families had grown close over the years, and closer still now that they were in-laws.

But not Daisy and Arabella.

"What time do we have to be at your dad's?" asked Daisy.

"Not until 6pm," Arabella replied, glancing down at her phone. "Maggie and Georgie arrived this morning, and they went out for a surf with Dad and Bill this afternoon, so they won't be home until at least half-past five."

Maggie and Georgie were twins, a few years older than Clem. They were both at university in Brisbane and often came down to see their dad and surf their local break.

The two families had arranged a barbecue at Jeff's house that evening to celebrate having five of their six kids in town. But first, Arabella and Daisy had planned to discuss what was happening with Garden and Bay.

The media interest in Daisy's stall had only increased in the week following her Hollywood encounter. Daisy had become something of an overnight celebrity - online anyway, and Arabella had been fielding calls from all sorts of websites and tabloids. Daisy and her shop assistant Sarah had been busy stuffing parcels to send out to their online customers and ordering in new stock. There had even been several more offers to buy out the company, including the incredibly generous offer from Thread Bare.

The company's CEO, Saffron Williams, had personally flown up to Byron to make the offer.

"We are genuinely impressed with the way you have developed your brand in tandem with your sustainable, conscious capitalist approach," she'd said smoothly, before offering Daisy an eye watering amount of money to buy the brand.

"I want you to know we are committed to this acquisition, Daisy. It's a win/win scenario for both of us. What you have achieved aligns perfectly with the Thread Bare ethos. Adding Garden and Bay to our portfolio will consolidate our position as the number one choice for the 18–30 socially conscious demographic. And your reputation as the architect of that branding will position you as the country's most in demand project manager, brand developer, designer, whatever it is you want to do next Daisy. With the added bonus of course, of getting to walk away with a very comfortable pay out."

"Take your time and think it over. Let's stay in touch and we can speak again in a few weeks." Saffron pushed a large stack of paperwork across the counter.

That had been yesterday.

Daisy had spent the last 24 hours in a daze, filling orders on autopilot and stopping every few minutes to look at the contract Saffron had left. Finally, she realised thinking about it was getting her nowhere and she called Arabella and asked her to meet her at the Gardiner's for a chat.

"So, how are you feeling about everything?" asked Arabella, looking contemplatively at her friend.

Daisy sat at the table silently, absentmindedly chewing on one of her fingernails. Elvis was curled up at her feet, his nose resting gently on one foot as she stroked his belly with the other.

"I don't know," she replied after a long pause.

"You know you don't have to sell if you don't want to. Just because it's a good offer doesn't mean you have to take it," said Arabella, taking a sip of her tea.

Daisy looked up at Arabella and sighed.

"It's a pretty good offer, isn't it? I mean, I'd be able to get the car fixed and pay Mum and Dad back the loan they gave me when I first opened the stall, which would help them with some of their other bills. Things are not good with them right now and I think they could really use the money. I'd be crazy not to think about it, wouldn't I?"

It was true. The offer from Thread Bare was quite generous for an unknown brand like Garden and Bay, and the cash injection would make Daisy and her family a little more comfortable.

Daisy thought about selling for a second and then looked up sadly. "But I don't know AB, I just don't know."

Arabella looked across at Daisy for a moment. "Do you want to know what I think?" she asked gently.

Daisy nodded.

"It was always your dream to work in fashion. And you found a way to make that happen, even if it wasn't the way you imagined. Of course, it would be hard to consider giving it up, because you've worked so hard on it."

Daisy pulled back and crossed her arms defensively. "I did what I had to do for Mum and Dad..." she began, but Arabella interrupted her.

"I know. And it was a really lovely thing you did. But maybe it is time you did something for yourself?"

"It's my baby, AB. I've worked so hard on this over the last six years. And I've always wanted to make fabric and design clothes. I'm already doing that right now. Why would I want to stop?" Daisy sighed before continuing. "But you're right. I've been saying for a while now that I need a change. The shop has been great, but it's not exactly what I thought I would end up doing. If I do sell, why shouldn't I hold out for more money? Because this is my future we are talking about. Or is that just being greedy? I don't know!"

Daisy stopped talking to catch her breath, her eyes flashing with uncertainty.

"Arabella, you know how hard things have been for Mum and Dad. This could be a real chance for me to help them out, after...after everything that's happened..."

Arabella reached out and squeezed Daisy's hand gently, but Daisy pulled her hand away. Things were not the same anymore.

"Your mum and dad love you, babe. They don't hold you responsible - you know that. And they certainly would never forgive themselves if they thought they were holding you back from doing something that you really wanted to do."

"You know what I really wish for?" Daisy asked finally. "I really wish I could just run away for a few weeks."

Arabella thought for a minute. "Well, why don't you? Sarah can run the stall without you for a few weeks and you can take care of the back end no matter where you are. Come down to the city and spend some time in Bondi with me and Royce. You can hang out at a different beach for a change and explore the city. A change of scenery might give you a whole new perspective on things."

Arabella paused. "I know Royce would love to spend some time with you. And I'd really like to have you stay for a while," she added, squeezing Daisy's hand again. "I miss having you around to talk to."

Daisy rolled the idea around her mind for a few minutes. A few weeks in Bondi might be fun. Take some time away from the shop and see how it felt to not be tethered to a business in the same town she had been born in. But it had been a long time since she and Royce and Arabella had spent time together. Would it be weird?

"I have to go," she said abruptly, before jumping down the back stairs and grabbing her bike.

Arabella nodded to the empty room. She knew Daisy was headed to the sand to watch the last of the day's light slip away and work through her decision. It's what she'd always done when there was a big choice to make. Arabella knew she'd find her way back eventually.

THREE

Oh-Em-Gee *Byron Bay might have been the place to be last week, but sources tell us the Watson brothers, Tilly Bingham and Ed Sheeran have since decamped for the warmer waters of Fiji. Exclusive photos of their private island beach party at the link in the bio!*

———

Down on the beach, Daisy watched as the sky grew darker. One by one, the stars popped out in the early night sky and the moon began to rise, its silver reflection dancing on the sea.

A few weeks ago, when she had gotten up to get a glass of water in the middle of the night, she'd overheard her parents bickering about money. Not fighting exactly–they never really fought–but the stress and fear was obvious in their hushed voices.

"The kids don't need to know. They are already

working too hard, and this is not something they need to worry about."

"Lola, I just wish you'd let me take on…"

"We've been over this. I can't let you make any more sacrifices. It's just not bloody fair."

"You're my wife. I want to make the sacrifices."

"I'm sure it will be fine. We'll make it work."

"We always seem to, don't we?"

Careful not to disturb her parents, Daisy crept back to her room and lay staring at the ceiling for the next few hours, her mind racing. Of course, it was money they were worried about. And she was the reason they were worried about money.

———

Sitting on the beach, Daisy thought back to that awful time, ten years ago, when she was just a kid, fresh out of high school.

She and Arabella had just graduated from high school and were leaving for university in Sydney the following week. They were excited and were spending their last days in Byron down on the beach or heading out to parties to say farewell to their friends. On their last Saturday night in town, there was a party on a property out on the road to Bangalow. It was raining and Arabella had stayed home that night, but Daisy had gone out anyway, eager to spend as much time with her boyfriend Jordan as possible.

Later in the evening, when the party was winding down, Daisy realised Jordan had been drinking, despite promising to be the designated driver for the night. She refused to get in the car with him and he drove off angrily, leaving her at the party alone. The festivities had well and truly ended by then, only a handful of unfamiliar faces were left sitting around the fire.

In a panic, she called her parents and Lola drove out to pick her up. The roads were slippery from all the rain and on the way home, Lola lost control of the car. It slid sideways and rolled down an embankment, wrapping around a tree and catching on fire. Luckily, no one else was involved, but Lola broke her leg and Daisy was seriously injured. They both needed several operations and months of rehabilitation. Things between Jordan and Daisy never recovered, and he left for uni not long after the accident. The last time Daisy saw him she was still in hospital.

The medical bills had been huge and once Daisy was able to come home, she needed constant care for another few months. Lola had to take time off work to recover and to look after Daisy, and without a second income, her parents were forced to take out a second mortgage. When Daisy had recovered and was slowly becoming more independent, Bill and Lola had partly financed the beginning of Garden and Bay. Daisy was determined to pay her parents back, but the business had been slow to take off, and she was only now able to start making serious inroads into her debt. But the damage had been done and Bill and Lola were now in debt for life.

After Daisy had recovered from her car accident, she felt terrible and stubbornly decided to stay in Byron to run the stall and work odd jobs at the pub, to help her parents out financially. She had attended a few classes at the local TAFE and discovered she shared her mum's talent for numbers, but she hadn't known what to do with it. For a long time now, she had been making decisions based on how she could help her parents stay financially stable in the short term.

They had sacrificed so much for her, and she knew things were harder for her parents than they let on. For Daisy, staying back in Byron to help her family was the least she could do. Then Covid hit. Somehow, they all made it through, but her dad was now working two jobs, while Lola had lost hers soon after, when the company she worked for went bust. She helped with the shop when she could, in between picking up backfill shifts here and there. But it all added up to financial pressure on the Gardiners that was bigger than ever and a blow the family didn't need.

Daisy sighed. Royce and Arabella had been great, helping as much as they could. But Arabella had her own family commitments, helping her father pay for Maggie and Georgie's school fees. They were all getting by, but there was not a lot of flexibility in their finances.

This sale really could change things for the whole extended family.

It could change things for her. There was a lot she had missed out on.

If she was honest, she was to blame for how awkward things had gotten between her and Arabella. She had watched AB and Royce thrive once they got to Sydney, getting great jobs, starting businesses, travelling the world for work. Falling in love. Leaving her behind.

That was meant to be my world too, she thought sadly. *But I stayed here for my family. I did the responsible thing. I pushed them away, didn't I? I think I've been jealous all this time and didn't know it.*

Daisy stood up and brushed the sand off her legs and walked purposefully down to the water's edge.

"Ok ocean," she whispered to the glittering water in front of her. "What do I do now?"

The water surged up around her ankles in answer before pulling away with a gentle hiss. "I guess some time away might be good for me," she replied, as she wandered along the hard sand, letting the cool sea water surge up and over her feet. "But how do you know when it's right?"

The ocean surged again in response and Daisy noticed a small object sparkling on the water's edge. Curious, she bent down to see what it was. An almost round piece of blue sea glass, about the size of a marble, sat shining on the sand. The ocean waves had polished it smooth and with the light of the moon flooding through; it looked more like a delicate little bubble than a solid chunk of glass.

As Daisy picked it up and watched in fascination, it seemed like entire worlds were rising and falling within the glass sphere. Beginnings and endings and beginnings.

"Ok, I see your point," she said, smiling wryly out at the glinting sea.

Maybe it really was time for a new beginning.

———

Later that night, Daisy made her way back home. The cicadas were humming in the warm night air as she walked up the stairs of Jeff's veranda and slipped onto the lounge beside her mum. She looked around at the faces of her extended family. They were lucky to have such a wonderful hometown. There was so much comfort in knowing it was always going to be there. But nothing stays the same forever. And Daisy had been busy standing still for ten years now.

Daisy rolled the piece of sea glass between her fingers. As she thought about her options and about the idea of spending some time in Sydney, something seemed to click into place. This was her chance to do something big...well maybe not big, but something. Sell or not, she really needed to know what else was out there. She needed to know if she could fit into a new world.

She looked over at Arabella and smiled. She was sitting at the table next to Clem, scrolling through her phone, both of them laughing hysterically. Once upon a time, Arabella and Royce had been her closest friends in the entire world. It wasn't that crazy, spending some time with them at their apartment in Bondi. Maybe it was time for them to reconnect. She could always jump on a plane and be home in just over an hour.

"Mum, Dad, can I talk to you for a second?" she asked, drawing them away from the others.

"What would you think about me going down to Sydney to stay with Arabella and Royce for a few weeks? I talked to Sarah, and she is happy to keep things running here. Can you please give her a hand when she needs it, Mum? Will you really be ok with just Clem helping around the house?"

Lola looked at her oldest daughter and smiled. "Of course, darling! We are not old fogies who need constant care. Besides, Clem is a great help when she is not off making those mad TikTok videos of hers."

"Are you really sure? I still don't know if I am going to sell or not, but I think this might be a good opportunity for me to clear my head and see if this is really what I want to be doing in my life. Do you think that's crazy? I really want to make sure I make the right decision because I could end up regretting it for the rest of my life. If I sell, I could pay you back everything I owe you and that might make things easier. Maybe this is a chance to make everything right finally."

Daisy had barely finished speaking before she found herself wrapped in the arms of her mother.

"Oh Daisy, come here. I love you so much. And I am really proud of you. You don't need to make anything right, love, you know that. You've grown up into such a great young woman. And I love how kind and thoughtful you are. But an adventure would be so good for you. You really do deserve more than you are letting yourself experience. And your dad and I will always be here for you, if you need us."

Daisy looked up at her dad. He smiled at her through his bushy beard and took her hand.

"Sweetheart, you've been punishing yourself for the accident for far too long. We don't expect you to pay us back. We are so proud of what you have achieved. Your mum and me are fine. We've got Clem and Jeff to look after us. It's time for you to go and do something new. Have some fun."

"But I heard what you said the other night, about the debts and the—"

"Listen here Daisy, you're the kid in this family! It's time you stopped worrying so much about us and started acting like one for a change. Go to Sydney."

Jeff's booming voice interrupted Bill. "Is that Daisy? Awesome, everyone is here. Time for a toast. Come on Gardiners, get over here."

Daisy, Bill, and Lola joined the others at the barbecue and raised their glasses to Jeff's toast.

"To family!" he pronounced, looking around at his daughters and his best friends with a grin. "No matter where they are in the world."

Daisy looked across at Arabella and nodded. Arabella lifted her glass to Daisy and smiled.

"You won't regret it Daisy, I promise!"

"What? What's going on?" asked Clem, looking from her mum to her dad, and to Arabella and Daisy.

Arabella stopped, a serious look on her face.

"Shit, I should tell Royce. He should be back by now; he's been covering the elections in Egypt this week. Give me a second, I'll get him on speaker..."

Daisy took a deep breath and held the sea glass bubble tight in her hand, while the loving chaos of her extended family enveloped her.

FOUR

WhathappensinBondi...*Reality TV darling Lozza Rothermere-Smythe and her best frenemy Prudencia Peterstone were spotted painting Bondi-town red last night. Lozza and Prudencia, stars of the breakout series Sydney Confidential, were spotted drinking champagne and arguing forcefully in the carpark outside the Pavilion, before heading up to a private function at Icebergs. Both were no-shows at their scheduled charity fundraiser in Rose Bay this morning— perhaps both ladies were too busy trying out this season's hottest hangover cure from Juicy Lucy? #oops!*

In what seemed like the blink of an eye, Daisy found herself settled in at Arabella and Royce's sunny beachside apartment. The Notts Avenue apartment block was arguably one of Bondi Beach's most sought-after properties, sitting high above the southern end of Australia's most famous beach, and just to the left of Australia's most famous swimming pool, the Icebergs Swimming Club. Royce and Arabella lived a life that others only dreamed about via their Instagram accounts and Daisy couldn't believe she was finally back here after so long.

While his band members had spent their money on the many pleasures of stardom, Royce had bought an apartment, which at the time was the most un-rock'n'roll thing he could've done. It was also the smartest thing he could've done. The band fell apart not long after, but Royce had used his connections to build up an impressive photojournalism portfolio, eventually cementing himself as one of Australia's most in demand news photographers.

Daisy was excited to be spending some time with her big brother. Aside from chaotic Christmases and the occasional birthday or anniversary party, it had been a long time since they had seen each other and just spent time together. As Daisy and Arabella had drifted apart, so too had Daisy and Royce. It had all felt so sad, yet inevitable. They still wrote long emails to each other every few months, and even though there had been a gap in their lives, Daisy was worried that the only reason she was able to leave the coast was because her big brother was waiting for her on the other side.

Daisy and Clem had a big heart to heart before they left for the airport.

"Clem, I need you to keep an eye on the folks for me, OK? I know they like to act all cool and tough, but money is tight for them right now."

"It's ok Daisy, I can look after them. You know how good I am at bossing them around! Besides, you're not going forever, right? I mean, you will come home soon, promise?"

"I promise!"

The two sisters had hugged tightly, and Clem agreed to keep Daisy updated every week.

"I'll message you so much you'll think you were still here," sniffed Clem.

Leaving Byron had been hard. If saying goodbye to Clem and her mum and dad had been tough, driving away from Elvis had been almost unbearable.

What a monumental sook I am! She thought ruefully. *I'm a few hours from home, not the other side of the world!*

Daisy shook her head, clearing her mind of home, and walked out onto the balcony to gaze at the vista before her.

Bondi Beach stretched out in front of the apartment, a pale arc of sand buffeted gently by a bay of undulating and sparkling water. A cool, salty breeze swept in from the north and Daisy couldn't help but shiver in delight.

"It's not a bad a view to come home to, is it?"

Daisy turned at the familiar voice of her brother. "Hey Royce," she smiled tentatively. "When did you get back?"

"Late last night," he replied, looking down at his sister, before stepping forward to hug her tightly.

"It is really good to see you, Daisy," he whispered. "It's been too long."

They hugged for a few more seconds before self-consciously pulling apart and looking back out over the beach.

"Has AB already left for work?" Royce asked.

"Yep, I heard her get up and go about 7:30am. "

"I must have been dead to the world. I remember

nothing since I fell into bed at about 3am last night. That was a killer flight delay. 26 hours in Dubai. I'm sorry I wasn't here when you girls got back from Byron."

Royce walked out into the sunshine on the balcony and tilted his head up into the sunshine.

"Oh man, it's good to be home!" he said, soaking in the rays. "Welcome to the Bondi bubble!"

Daisy looked up at her brother basking in the sun, and a wave of affection swept over her. Royce was not quite two years older than Daisy, and from a distance, they were often mistaken for twins. Both had bright green eyes and brown curly hair, and the same tilted nose and dimpled chin they had inherited from their mum. But while Daisy was a respectable 5ft 8, Royce hadn't stopped growing until he was 6ft 2, towering over all the women in the family and topping his dad by several inches. Daisy had always adored her handsome brother, mostly, as she was so fond of telling him, because he reminded her so much of herself. She had missed him over the last few years.

"Have you had breakfast?" Royce asked once he had soaked up enough sun. "We should walk up to North Bondi and have a swim on the way back."

"Great, I'm starved! Let's go!"

Royce and Daisy followed the winding, uneven steps down to the promenade that stretched out along the curve of the beach. Chatting excitedly, they wandered north, past the skate ramp and lifesaver's tower and the buttery yellow Bondi Surf Pavilion. Once upon a time, the stately old structure had contained bathing compartments and tea rooms and a war time Officer's Club. These days it housed coffee shops and hip bars, as well as yoga classes and a community centre. Despite many changes over the years, it was still one of the most iconic parts of the beachside suburb.

As they wandered along in the early morning sun, Daisy marvelled at the already packed beach. The smell of sunscreen and salt water washed over her, but despite the familiar fragrance, it all seemed so different to home, where things were much more casual. Here, everyone seemed desperate to be seen. Up above, busloads of tourists posed for endless selfies. Carloads of young muscle boys drove laps up the one-way street, blasting out the latest Spotify mix. On the sand below them sat hundreds of people in all shapes and all sizes, most of them in very little clothing. Stripy umbrellas and fluorescent pineapple prints filled the beach. Wannabe supermodels strolled up and down in denim cut offs, bikini tops and round lens sunglasses, a coffee cup clutched in hand, and a mobile phone in the other. Bronzed Brazilian boys in barely-there lycra briefs were playing beach volleyball. One of them winked at Daisy as she strolled by, causing her eyes to widen and her cheeks to warm.

Daisy was so entranced by the action that she didn't see the dog before it was too late. The little ball of blue fur jumped up excitedly and ran between Daisy's legs, causing her to stumble and land awkwardly on her left knee. A decent sized graze zigzagged across her skin. Daisy sat, dazed for a second, brushing sand out of the already stinging cut, hindered by an enthusiastic dog licking her face, desperate for a pat.

Down below, the Brazilians sniggered at the sight of the fallen girl, before turning their attention back to their game.

"Oh man, I'm so sorry!" said the dog's horrified owner, standing over the equally mortified Daisy. "Get away from her, you mad dog!" he cried, pushing the blue heeler away. "Are you ok?"

Daisy looked up into the most beautiful brown eyes she had ever seen. Her eyes travelled over his tanned face, broad shoulders and long lean legs, only to confirm that the rest of him was equally beautiful.

Suddenly, Daisy realised she was still sitting on the ground with a bleeding knee, staring at a cute guy. *Oh man,* she groaned to herself. *I look so stupid right now!*

She gratefully took his outstretched hand and stood, feeling the sting of the graze as she straightened her knee.

"I am so sorry!" Daisy said. "Is that your dog? Is it ok?"

"Yes, that is my good-for-nothing dog Costello. She's fine. My name's Dan, otherwise known as mortified dog owner."

Dan looked down at his dog, who was now laying on the cool concrete at Dan's feet.

"You are a bad, bad dog Costy, you know that right?" he said, affectionately shaking his head at his very relaxed dog.

Costello responding with a loving lick to Dan's bare foot.

Daisy laughed. "Costello, no way!"

Dan looked at her quizzically.

"I have a dog. His name is Elvis," Daisy explained and held out her hand again. "I'm Daisy"

"Nice to meet you Daisy," said Dan.

"Are you an Elvis fan too?

"No, actually, we used to have another dog. They were

an inseparable duo, Howard and Costello…my grand-mother was a lifetime member of Liberal Party," Dan replied with a sheepish grin.

Royce watched the endearingly awkward exchange and laughed to himself.

"Ahh, my sister," he said, choosing his words carefully. "Falling over and befriending every animal since the Nineties. Hey man, I'm Royce, Daisy's brother."

He looked down at Daisy with an affectionate grin.

"Come one, let's get you down to the water and wash that graze off."

"Bye Dan, bye Costello!" said Daisy, as she leant on her brother and slowly made her way down the beach.

She looked back over her shoulder from the sand and smiled, as Dan shook his head at his wayward dog.

"Why do you always pick the cute ones to trip over? You know hurting them is not the way to impress them, right?" he said.

Costello put her paw over her eyes for a second in response, before being distracted by three small boys with handfuls of hot chips.

"Come on, you mad dog, let's get you home."

———

After Daisy's knee had been cleaned up, she and Royce limped up to Speedos Café at the northern end of the beach. They were lucky to get a seat straight away at the small, perennially busy café next door to the North Bondi RSL. They ordered coffees and smashed avo and eggs on toast and sat back to admire the ever-changing blue sea and busy beach.

"So, I hear you have a pretty big decision to make," observed Royce, shifting his attention back to his sister after a few moments of silent contemplation.

Daisy sighed. "Yeah. It's pretty scary," she admitted, relieved to finally be talking to her brother about the big decision she was facing.

"You know, sometimes I just can't believe how lucky I was to have made the decision to buy my apartment," mused Royce. "Do you remember how scared I was about committing so much money? Sometimes I could just kiss past me for having the good sense to go ahead with the purchase."

"Remember how Mum and Dad were so horrified? They were like 'Royce, no one will ever want to buy a fancy apartment in Bondi...you'll never sell it!' Now look at you... you're a bloody millionaire!"

Royce laughed. "Hardly a millionaire sister. We would be if we sold it, but between helping out back home and keeping up with the body corporate fees, we rarely even have money put aside for savings."

Daisy's smile faded as she thought of the pressure she had caused for her family. But Royce jumped in quickly, as though he knew immediately what she was thinking about.

"Stop thinking that! It is not a problem ...you know we'd do this all over again in a heartbeat for you and for the family. You can't let what happened ten years ago be a factor in your decision."

Daisy smiled gratefully and turned the conversation back to Royce. "I thought things were going really well for you guys?" she asked curiously, as the waitress delivered their coffees.

"Oh, it is. Don't get me wrong, I've got steady work and AB's company is one of the best in the country." Royce paused for a moment, and Daisy could almost see him reflecting back on the life he and his wife had built in Sydney. "It's just a bloody expensive life to maintain!" he continued, running a hand through his unruly hair. "AB's company is just starting to break even. And she has to dress the part every day. Her job is all about projecting the right image you know, so she has to have the right clothes and the right hair. She's lucky she can borrow outfits from her designer friends when she needs to."

Royce looked out at the ever-changing procession of beautiful people strolling past the café.

"I'm glad we can keep up the façade of being successful. But it just goes to show you never really know what is going on behind the scenes," he added thoughtfully.

Daisy nodded in agreement. "Yeah, Mum and Dad sure make it look like they have it all together."

"You and AB seem to be getting along ok," Royce observed carefully. "Do you think you will be ok hanging out together?!

Daisy looked down at her coffee for a minute, thinking of the right words to say. "Yeah, I think so. I mean, it's not like we ever had a big falling out. We just stopped hanging out. It got hard, you guys were so far away, and I was in my own little world back home."

She looked up at him and smiled. "I think it was the right time to make amends. I am really happy to be here with you both."

As their food was delivered, their conversation turned to news and stories from home and the siblings were soon engrossed in family gossip. Royce watched his sister carefully as she caught him up on Clem's latest escapades and Elvis' trip to the vet.

"I'm really glad you're here Daisy," he said, smiling down at his sister. "Things have been a bit weird lately and I think you might be just what we needed."

———

Later that night, as Royce, Arabella and Daisy sat around the table out on the balcony, Royce couldn't help but tease his little sister.

"So Daisy met a boy today," he laughed, winking at his wife mischievously.

Arabella grinned back. "Oh really? Already? Gee, that was fast!"

"Yes, his name is Dan, and he has a dog called Costello, after Howard and Costello!" continued Royce with a smirk.

"Really Daisy? How very Eastern Suburbs of you! You know, I never pegged you for the type that would fall for a right-winger!" teased Arabella.

Daisy blushed bright red at their gentle teasing. *What was with all this blushing today?* she thought to herself. *Get a grip Gardiner!*

In years gone by, this would have been just another night the three of them spent together. But while Daisy was feeling like it was old times again, she was still cautious and crossed her arms defensively.

Royce noticed her hesitation. He gently nudged her under the table and winked at her.

"Stop it, you two! It wasn't like that at all. I just fell over and looked stupid, and he felt bad."

"Uh huh... that is exactly what happened," countered Royce with a laugh. "That and the googly eyes you were both making at each other."

Royce's sister and wife both turned to look at him, teasing smiles flashing across their faces.

"Googly eyes? Really? That's lame, even for you, darling!" chortled Arabella.

"Yeah, your dad jokes are getting worse and worse these days!" As Daisy rushed to turn the tables on her big brother, she didn't notice Arabella's expression or how quickly she changed the subject.

"Hey enough about Royce, we need to talk about you and the shop," said Arabella, pouring another glass of wine for Daisy and her husband. "How are you feeling about it all?"

"I don't know! I'm still so unsure about what to do," replied Daisy with a sigh. "I love Garden and Bay, I really do, and I love creating things. But it's not what I thought I would end up doing forever. I'm so lucky Thread Bare have given me a grace period to think about it because I don't know what I should do, and I really need figure it out."

Daisy leant forward and rested her chin on her palm and gazed at Royce and Arabella.

"What do you guys think I should do?"

Arabella and Royce exchanged glances before Arabella spoke. "We don't want to tell you what to do... you have to make that decision yourself. But we can give you some different perspectives, you know, as outsiders. Help you identify your options."

Arabella looked at Daisy and smiled. "I actually think you are in a great position. Thread Bare has made you a solid offer. You could take that, and it will sort out all your immediate troubles. You could take time off, figure out what to do next. But, if you decide you want to keep the shop, you could build on the publicity that you have received and use it to build a bigger business. You have always wanted to make Garden and Bay more of a fashion label, rather than just a stall and an online shop."

Arabella paused and looked at Royce for a second before continuing.

"If you were my client, I would tell you to spend some time building your personal brand. That would mean that you might increase the asking price for the business if you decide to sell, as well as keep your business in the public's mind if you decide not to."

"But I wouldn't want to hold out and increase the price. Should I do that?" asked Daisy, confused. "I mean, Thread Bare have been so great and I already have a relationship with them. It would be kind of mean when they have been so nice about waiting for my decision. Plus, I have to think about Sarah. Thread Bare have promised she won't lose her job in the sale."

"I think Arabella's seeing this from the perspective of her nine-to-five life Daisy, which is not necessarily about right or wrong. We all know sometimes Arabella's job has a little bit of a different moral compass than those of us who live in the real world."

Oof, thought Daisy, looking at Royce and Arabella.

Arabella was looking at her husband with raised eyebrows. *That was a bit mean...especially for Royce.*

"Don't look at me like that, either of you! I don't mean that AB has no moral compass! Just that her line of business sometimes has a different way of looking at the world and the things that matter in that world are often not what matters in the rest of the world."

Royce yawned before continuing. "Look, all I am saying is that the fashion and celebrity world is not always that nice. People can be jerks and you are a nice person, Daisy. You are kind and sweet and I worry that if you decided to keep the stall and try your luck as a fashion designer, these people will chew you up and spit you out again."

Arabella choked on her drink. "Dude! I know you don't always love my job and that sometimes you think it's all superficial, but that's really negative and so unfair on Daisy. You know she is smart and tough. She's managed tougher times than the fashion industry!"

"Sorry babe, I'm tired and not explaining myself very well. The jet lag is catching up with me. I'm going to hit the sack and let you two finish chatting about this." Royce tiredly got up and kissed his wife and sister goodnight.

"Daisy, I'll support you no matter what you decide to do...none of these decisions are bad. It's just going to come down to how you want to move forward in your life. Look, I'm helping a friend at a shoot here in the city in a few days. Why don't you come along and see what you think? Have a chat with a few people about the industry."

Arabella smiled tightly as Royce walked inside and took another sip of her sparkling water. She was on a three-day detox and was drinking soda water out of a wine glass, so she didn't feel left out. It didn't seem to do much, but keep Arabella in a perpetually cranky mood.

"What would building my personal brand actually mean?" Daisy asked, turning the topic back to a safer area.

"Well, you'll just be you, but in Bondi and around town in Sydney. You won't have to do anything unusual, except come out with me to a few fun parties...and I promise there will be real champagne there!" Arabella laughed, gesturing to her glass.

"I'll give you a list of the cool bars and cafes to be seen at here in Bondi and you just keep being your gorgeous and earthy self, practicing yoga down at the beach, running, surfing, nothing you don't already do every day, anyway. We'll fire up your Instagram with lots of fun, healthy beach pics. And I'll make sure photos of you get into the right publications and I'll mention to a few of the columnists that you are staying with me while you are in town negotiating a big deal. Sydney Fashion Festival is coming up too, a fortnight of fashion showcases and parties. I can take you to the opening party and to as many shows as you like and introduce you to a few hot designers. See if you like it. And over the next few weeks, your brand will be solidified, and your business traffic will continue to increase, which will only make your sale price rise—should you choose to negotiate for a higher price."

Arabella glanced inside the flat pensively.

"Listen, you think about it. There's no rush. But I should get in there and check on my husband. He hasn't been this grumpy in ages...maybe he's getting sick, poor guy."

After Arabella had said goodnight, Daisy sat back and

looked out over the dark bay. She didn't feel any closer to knowing what it was she should do. Or what she wanted to do. But it felt good to have Arabella explaining it to her. And it felt good to have Royce looking out for her too, even if he and Arabella didn't exactly see eye to eye on the matter. It was exactly how it had been when they were kids —Arabella dreaming up all the ideas, Royce keeping her feet on the ground and Daisy leading the charge into the next adventure. Until the accident changed everything.

I guess it couldn't hurt to follow AB's advice, she thought to herself, as she listened to the ocean crashing and hissing below her. *I mean, how bad could it be?*

————

The next morning, Daisy set off down the coastal track to Bronte for a run, mulling over Arabella and Royce's advice as she jogged along the picturesque coastal pathway. Starting from Icebergs in Bondi, the track wound its way south, down into the bays and then up onto the cliff tops of Tamarama, Bronte and Clovelly, all the way to Coogee and beyond, giving walkers a bird's-eye view of the rocks pools and the sandstone cliffs rising spectacularly out of the surging crystal and aqua water below. As she ran, Daisy tried to imagine what she would do if she wasn't managing her shop. But it was no use. She just didn't know. So she turned up the music on her phone and surged forward. If she wasn't going to meditate, then she was going to work out!

She was hot and sweaty by the time she got back to

Bondi and as she reached the top of the stairs next to Icebergs, she stopped to catch her breath and admire the view. A familiar wet tongue licked her shin, and she looked down to see Costello, the dog from the beach yesterday, smiling up at her.

"Costello! Where are you, girl? Come here!"

Something inside Daisy's belly flip-flopped at the sound of that familiar voice and she looked across the dead-end street at the guy she hadn't been able to stop thinking about since they had met yesterday.

"It's ok, she's over here with me."

"I'm so sorry," Dan said, slamming the door of his truck and crossing the road to where Daisy and Costello were standing on the footpath. He looked down at his dog, who was staring up at Daisy. "She really likes you!"

"That's ok," laughed Daisy, bending down to scratch the little dog behind her ears. "The feeling is very mutual!"

"It's Daisy, right? Are you heading out down the track," asked Dan, gesturing down the pathway towards Tamarama.

"Actually no, I'm just coming back," said Daisy, mentally thanking him for not paying any attention to her sweaty, blotchy face.

"Are you ok? How's your leg?"

"Oh it's totally fine, just a scratch, see!" Daisy rolled up the hem of her three-quarter leggings to show off the small red scuff mark that was all that remained after yesterday's collision.

Dan smiled in relief. "I'm glad you're ok. But can I buy you a coffee anyway, just to say sorry? I've just finished up a survey and I've got a bit of time before I have to get to the next site."

"Sure!" said Daisy, "That would be great."

Daisy, Dan and Costello wandered down the path to the Codde Hole, the hole in wall café that overlooked the Icebergs pool.

As they ordered and took a seat, Daisy asked curiously "What do you do for work? What were you surveying this morning?"

"I'm the Coastal Ecology Project Coordinator for the local council," explained Dan. "Basically, me and my team make sure that all the beaches and parks are full of local, native plants and animals and that invasive species don't take over. That's what we've been doing this morning, surveying for an introduced weed called sea spurge."

"Wow! That is a really cool job!" replied Daisy, before crinkling her nose in mock disgust. "But what a gross name!"

"It's a great plant really," replied Dan with a laugh. "It's just not meant to grow here in Sydney."

As Dan explained the ins and outs of his job caring for the coastal areas of Waverly Council, their conversation flowed easily. Costello curled up for a sunny nap on Daisy's feet.

Suddenly, a balding man in a fisherman's vest was standing in front of them. Costello immediately stood up, hackles raised, and began growling at him.

"Hey Daisy, give us a smile!" the man called, aiming a large camera at their table. "And call your dog off, I'm not going to hurt ya!"

"Umm, why are you photographing us?" asked Daisy, smiling nervously and looking across at Dan in confusion.

"You're Daisy Gardiner, right? From Byron? Wayne from Elite Images. Don't worry love, this one's on us!" the man looked at his camera. "It's a great shot, you'll love it!

Daisy doubted it. She was still red faced and sweaty from her run, but she was too surprised to protest.

As soon as the photographer had taken his shot and walked away, Dan turned to Daisy with a quizzical look in his eye.

"Are you famous?" he asked carefully. "I mean, I didn't think so. I don't recognise you from anywhere. Plus, I figured most Bondi socialites wouldn't be caught dead having coffee with a scruffy ecologist like me." Dan paused and glanced down at his muddy work uniform. "And smelly," he laughed ruefully, shaking his head. "I promise I'll be a bit more presentable the next time I see you."

Daisy's stomach flip-flopped. *There's going to be a next time?* She thought, stifling an excited grin,

"Famous? Me? Oh no!" she said instead, gesturing to her well-worn t-shirt, one of her first prototypes, and op shop pants. "I mean, I'm not sure too many celebs would be seen dead in something this old! But it's comfy and easy to run in."

Daisy looked up at his crinkly brown eyes and was glad when they crinkled even more as he smiled back at her.

"Actually, I'm staying with my brother and his wife, Arabella. I run a little shop in Byron that got Instagrammed by a celebrity recently, and a big company offered to buy me out. So, I'm taking some time out, trying to figure out if I should sell it or not."

"Yeah, wow, that's pretty big," Dan replied. "What do you sell in your shop?"

"I make t-shirts, pyjamas, scarves and accessories from organic cotton and recycled fabric. It's not a huge business but I am really proud of it."

"Yeah, that is cool. You should be proud."

Dan smiled down at her again and this time Daisy's heart skipped a beat.

"So what do you think you'll do?" he asked, curiously.

"I dunno!" laughed Daisy ruefully. "The thing is, I'm not sure what it is I really want to do. You know, in my life. I kind of fell into the whole shop thing. I started working at a market stall and eventually got the chance to buy it from the original owner, and it grew into my little business."

Daisy looked up at Dan, her eyes shining at the thought of her little Byron empire.

"I just don't know if that is what I want to be doing for the rest of my life."

Daisy looked across at Dan shyly. "Is your job what you thought you'd end up doing?" she asked. "Is it your dream?"

Dan shook his head and laughed. "My grandmother was convinced I was going to be a scientist. I spent my entire childhood taking things apart and mixing things together, just to figure out how it all worked! I guess working in environment is kind of similar - I got to study science and learn how it all works and then when I realised how amazing everything is, I realised how much I wanted to protect it all!"

"I know that feeling...well at least the amazingness and wanting to protect it part. Some mornings when I am out for an early surf back home, when the sun is rising over the water and the colours are changing and the sun shines right through, it's such a perfect moment. And then I'll see some rubbish on the beach on my way home and the moment is broken. How can people be so unaware of what is happening right around us?" replied Daisy thoughtfully.

Dan was quiet for a moment as he thought about Daisy's question. It was the question he asked himself every week when he was fishing plastic out of the sea or re-planting a native shrub that had been trampled on by tourists desperate for that perfect Eastern Suburbs selfie.

Suddenly, he looked down at his watch.

"Oh crap, I am so late…I was meant to be back at the workshop 10 minutes ago! I have to go!" he said, gathering his things and standing up. "But hey, what are you doing in the morning?"

"No plans," replied Daisy. "It's kind of fun, this whole being on holiday and sorting your life out thing!"

"There is meant to be a nice offshore wind tomorrow and the swell coming through should be pretty smooth. You surf right? Want to come out with me in the morning? I've got a spare board you can use."

"I'd love to!" replied Daisy, relieved that she would get to see him again so soon. Sure, she liked the way his crinkly eyes made her feel, especially when he smiled down at her. But more than that, he was so easy to talk to. It had been a long time since she had met a guy she felt this comfortable with.

They made plans to meet at the north end of the beach at 5am, before Dan looked at his watch again.

"Damn it! I'm really late! I have to go! Come on Costello! See you tomorrow, Daisy."

Daisy watched Dan and Costello walk back up the rocky stairs to where his car was parked, a goofy grin plastered across her face.

I think I am really going to like it here, she thought to herself happily.

———

Later that day, as the sun was setting over the horizon, Daisy met Arabella back down at Icebergs for an early evening yoga class.

"It's so great to come home to the beach at the end of a long day," Arabella said appreciatively, putting down her various bags and folders and looking out over the water as the rosy glow of sunset turned the waves pink and orange. But despite breathing in the salty twilight air, she seemed distracted, and Daisy glanced at her friend in concern. Something was not right with Arabella.

"So did you like my little paparazzi present today?" Arabella asked finally, turning back to Daisy, a mischievous grin replacing her earlier quiet contemplation.

"You sent that photographer? Arabella! I was mortified! I can't believe you did that...and in front of Dan too!"

"Yes, I was going to ask about the dude in the photo...so that's Dan? He's quite handsome!"

"Yeah, he's also lovely! I'd like to not scare him off too much!" Daisy stopped and took a deep breath. "I mean, I think we might be friends, that's all," she said softly.

Arabella looked at Daisy carefully and reached over to squeeze her hand.

"It's ok you know. It's ok to like someone and want to get to know them," she said, serious for a moment.

Daisy studied the ground for a second, the familiar feelings of denial and resentment rising within her. But for the first time in a long time the feelings vanished just as quickly as they came, and she looked up her friend and smiled.

"Yeah, I know. I actually can't wait to see him again," Daisy replied. It felt good to say it out loud, so she squeezed Arabella's hand in return.

"Ok, this may be a bad time to tell you we are also getting photographed for the Daily Tele tonight. I'm helping Asha, the yoga teacher, out with some free publicity and this will also be great for you as well!" Arabella laughed at Daisy's expression. "Come on, it will be fun! Here, mind my stuff while I get changed!"

After the class had finished, the two girls lay on their mats, relishing their post-yoga calm. Daisy started to stretch and get up, but Arabella reached out and grabbed her arm. "Hey listen, can you stay here for a minute?"

"Sure, what's up?"

"Just stay with me for a minute, will you?"

The two friends lay side by side in the twilight, silently gazing up at the stars.

"I'm really glad you are here Daisy," Arabella began, her voice wavering a little. "I mean, here in Bondi. I have really hated not having you as a friend over these last few years. And I think I need you now more than ever. I really need to talk to someone."

Daisy sat up and looked at Arabella in concern. She had been right; something was going on with Arabella.

"Arabella, what's going on?" she asked worriedly.

Arabella looked up at Daisy and her eyes filled with tears.

"Oh Daisy, I'm so scared," she sobbed. "I'm fucking pregnant, and I don't know what to do!"

Five

Oh-Em-G *New girl in town Daisy Gardiner has been making the most of Bondi's beachside bliss. Click the link in our bio above for photos of Bondi's reluctant influencer and get the scoop on how she keeps her skin oh-so-fresh-as-a-daisy! #bondibabe #skinsofresh*

———

Fresh as a daisy? Daisy groaned to herself a week later, as she sat on the balcony in the sun scanning through Garden and Bay's social media accounts. She had been trying to decide between a swim, a run or a smoothie, but Oh Em G's hilarious description made her feel a little rebellious, so she ordered a burger and chips instead.

It's so ridiculous, she laughed ruefully. *I don't even have a skin care regime. I'm pretty sure they'd be horrified if they knew the truth!*

The last seven days had sped by in a blur of activity. It

had all started with Arabella's shock announcement. After she had stopped crying, Arabella had explained everything to Daisy.

"Royce and I agreed we would wait a few more years before thinking about kids. We are both working so hard right now, and it just doesn't feel right. We're not ready."

Arabella paused and took a deep breath. "I'm not ready."

Without thinking, Daisy had reached over to take hold of Arabella's hand. Arabella squeezed it back gratefully.

"So, what do you want to do?" Daisy asked gently.

"I don't know," replied Arabella softly. "I want a baby. Just not yet."

She looked up at Daisy. "I've been going crazy these last few weeks. I wanted to talk to you about this so bad. I felt so alone." She looked up at Daisy glumly. "I miss us."

Daisy moved closer and put her arms around her friend.

"I miss us too. I'm sorry that I let so much time go by. I think I was a little jealous. And really scared."

"I get it. I'm sorry we didn't make more effort to stay in touch. Life just gets busy, you know? But it shouldn't get in the way of family and friends."

Daisy and Arabella smiled shyly at each other in the early evening gloom.

"Well, that is all in the past, right? I'm here now and we can work this out. Have you told Royce yet?"

Arabella shook her head. "No, that is part of the problem. He is so excited about the idea of having kids. If it was up to him, we would have started years ago. He only agreed to wait because I asked him to. I am really scared to tell him, because he is going to want to jump in to this headfirst and I am not sure if I want to go through with it."

Daisy hugged AB closer.

"Royce is a good guy. He will understand and support you, whatever you decide."

AB nodded. "I know, but he would be so sad. And I don't want to hurt him. And I do want us to have a family, Daisy, I really do. But it's too soon. And I am just so scared."

"We'll figure it out AB. We always do," Daisy replied, hugging her friend again.

Arabella hugged her friend back. "I am so glad you are here."

———

Shortly after her heart to heart with Daisy, Arabella had finally plucked up the courage to tell her husband about the baby. And while Royce was ecstatic, Arabella was still unconvinced.

"Daisy, what if I'm not ready to have a baby? How do I know if this is the right thing to do?" she had said several times since the yoga class. "It's not a good time in my career, plus I am nowhere near healthy enough. And to be honest, I'm a little worried that I would still rather have a glass a wine. That is not the right way to start someone's life!"

But over the course of the week, as Royce became more and more excited about having a family, Arabella was getting used to the idea.

"At the very least," she whispered to Daisy, a few days

after she told Royce, "I might never have to cook again!" Royce had taken over the kitchen and was making sure Arabella ate her way through several boxes of fruit and vegetables every few days.

Aside from the baby excitement, Daisy had been busy taking advantage of the glorious weather and Bondi's relaxed and active lifestyle. *I guess I am going to have to go home one day soon, so I may as well enjoy having some time off, and it's not like I'm lying around binge watching tv all day!*

The truth was, Daisy had worked hard over the last few years. It was really nice to be taking a break, even if it was unexpected, and she was making sure she made the most of it.

Royce had taken her along to a photo shoot for a department store's national ad campaign that a friend of his was shooting and Daisy had sat quietly, observing the organised chaos of the shoot. She watched in wonder as Lex and Royce effortlessly coordinated the small army of makeup artists, set designers, fashion stylists, models, and company executives present on set in an old warehouse just south of the city. The sounds of the Ramones had blasted through the air as they worked, turning the crumbling old brick building into a stylised Cold War-era spy den.

During a shooting break, Daisy had walked up and down the racks of clothes, revelling in the different textures and colours of the garments hanging ready for the next scene. When they were all back on set, she watched, fascinated, as the stylists moved and retired and adjusted the outfits, pressing a crease here and fluffing out a skirt there. Daisy shivered every time the big white studio lights popped and whined, signalling a mad scramble to reset the studio. It was an exciting day which left Daisy with more questions than answers, but at least she felt she was on the right track finally.

When the shoot was packed down and the warehouse had returned to its original dark and dingy state, Royce and Daisy stood silently next to the remaining cases to be carried out to the car.

Royce turned to his sister. "Oh shit," he said, a slow grin spreading across his face. "I'm going to be a dad!" He sat down on one of the equipment cases with a thud.

Daisy laughed. "Are you only just realising that now?" she teased, taking a seat next to Royce and slipping her arm through his. "How are you feeling about it all?"

"You know what, it's not the most ideal time for me and Arabella. I mean, I think I always had this idea that we would be in a much better place before we started having kids. But we haven't ever really talked about it, so I guess that was all in my head."

Royce paused and looked down at his sister. "But Daisy, I don't think I have ever been so happy about anything in my life! This kid, this baby already means more to me than I could possibly imagine. It's the weirdest and best feeling."

"Have you told Arabella that?"

Royce's expression changed at the mention of his wife's name.

"I get she is scared and worried. I feel like such a jerk being so excited about it when she is still so unsure. I mean, she is the one who has to change her whole life and her whole body for this to happen. She has every right to call the shots. But I am so happy that this has happened."

Daisy patted Royce's knee affectionately and stood up.

"You're a good guy Royce Gardiner. And you are going to be the best dad ever! You and Arabella will work it out, I know you will. I'm really happy for you guys and I can't wait to meet my first niece or nephew!"

———

While Arabella and Royce were busy figuring out their unexpected new adventure in parenting, Daisy was busy getting to know Dan.

As planned, they met up the morning after their unexpected coffee date for an early surf. Daisy joined Dan out the front of the North Bondi Surf Club and eagerly checked out his spare board.

"Nice curves," she said, running her hands down the fibreglass sides admiringly.

"I wasn't sure how comfortable you would be out on the water, so I thought we would start off up this end, where things are a bit more relaxed," Dan explained. "See Ben Buckler over there, the headland? That keep things a little more protected than further down the beach..."

Dan broke off as Daisy dropped her towel and took off running down the sand. "Come on then, let's get out there!" she shouted over her shoulder as she charged for the water.

For a moment Dan stood still as he watched Daisy run effortlessly into the water and slide onto the board. It only took her a couple of minutes to paddle out behind the break. Pretty soon she was in the lineup, jostling for a wave with some of the other locals. Dan chucked his towel down beside Daisy's and quickly jogged to the water to join her.

"Oh snap," he called out, once he had caught up to Daisy. "You didn't tell me you were so good. What else are you hiding?"

For the next hour they had competed good naturedly, trying to out-snake each other every time a good set rolled through. Daisy was clearly in her element and Dan was clearly mesmerised by how much she loved being out on the water.

"You look good out here Daisy, almost like a local," he teased when they stopped for a breather in between waves. "Not bad for a northerner blow in!"

Daisy wiped the salty water from her eyes and sat up straight for a moment, taking a deep breath in the morning sunshine. She felt the cool ocean surge up and down as she gently bobbed on the sea green water. It was her happy place. Her comfort place. Her home.

Opening her eyes, she looked across at the guy bobbing beside her. He looked so good in the water, his dark hair slicked back, saltwater rivulets sliding down his collarbone. Even from this distance, she could see a dusting of freckles on each of his shoulders, and it took all of her strength not to reach out to touch them, one by one.

"You're not too bad yourself," she teased in reply. "You know, for a city boy!"

Get a grip Gardiner, she thought, shaking her head and trying not to laugh. Instead, she looked around and saw the next wave rise from the depths.

"Come on, I'll race you back to shore. Loser buys

breakfast!" Daisy peeled off suddenly, taking Dan by surprise.

"Ooh, that one is a bloody live one, mate," one of the other surfers called out behind him.

Nah, she's not a live one, he thought to himself as he happily paddled after her. *She's bloody amazing.*

———

Since that first morning's surf, Daisy and Dan had been seeing each other almost every day. If the waves were good, they would meet on the sand early in the morning, before the beach got too busy and surf until Dan needed to go to work. They had also started meeting up for sundowners later in the day. Daisy had met Dan at a few of Bondi's ubiquitous bars, where he had introduced her to his friends. She had enjoyed meeting them and feeling like she was part of the Bondi 'It Crowd'. There was Louie, a local tradie who built sustainable, eco-friendly houses for rich people in the Eastern Suburbs and his model/wellness blogger girl-friend Fern. Daisy also met Dan's best friend James, an artist and surfboard shaper with a workshop and store in North Bondi.

Together the five of them had taken part in a commu-nity tree planting on the headland and had spent a morning at the Bondi Markets, running a reusable coffee mug and plate stall with a local environment group. They had even met up for coffee a few times at James' workshop, which made Daisy feel like she was living in Home and Away. All in all, it had been an interesting week and Daisy was feeling right at home in the little beachside suburb.

The only catch was that, while Arabella's plan to build her profile seemed to be very successful, Daisy could see that it made Dan uncomfortable whenever the cameras were out.

"Don't mind Dan," Fern had said conspiratorially, one morning when the cameras seemed to be following them more than usual and Dan was hiding out inside James' workshop. "He can be grumpy when he feels like things are not going the way he wants them to. He yells at me sometimes too, when Louie comes to my photo shoots and doesn't go surfing with him and James. Just ignore him, that's what I do!"

While Daisy had acted on Fern's advice and had so far been able to keep both parts of her life separate, it was getting harder and harder to ignore the photographers that seemed to follow her around wherever she went. Arabella had waved her magic public relations wand and Daisy was feeling like a celebrity, albeit a very minor league one. Thanks to Arabella's strategic patronage, Daisy had made it into the social pages of several newspapers, as well as some celebrity gossip and lifestyle websites and blogs.

Oh-Em-G was running a story about how to get glowing, healthy skin like Daisy, while the Daily Telegraph had profiled Garden and Bay in its Body and Soul section. Although Daisy was puzzled by Sydney's infatuation with the 'wellness' movement, where every green smoothie was considered some kind of badge of honour, her reputation as a nice, wholesome boho babe was growing fast.

So far, most photos had been taken at yoga or down on the beach after a surf and Daisy's healthy image was definitely keeping Thread Bare interested. Saffron Williams had called Daisy and assured her that their offer was good until the end of the month. She had even offered a few extra incentives to help Daisy choose their company.

The best thing about the whole situation, aside from getting to spend some quality time with Royce and Arabella, was that her sudden minor celebrity status meant sales through her online shop had been holding steady since Tilly's Instagram post. It also meant a few more offers had come in to buy the business. Arabella and Daisy had gone over the numbers, and it seemed that Arabella's predictions were accurate—as Daisy's profile grew, so too did her profits and the offers to buy her company. No matter what her decision was, Garden and Bay was going to be worth more if she held out for a few weeks.

There was only one dark cloud on the horizon. Clem had called Daisy and Royce in a panic after overhearing Bill and Lola talking about their mortgage repayments.

"It's bad, you guys," whispered Clem over the phone, before yelping quietly.

"Where are you?" asked Royce, puzzled at his youngest sister's antics.

"I'm in the shed—it's the only place in the whole house where you can have a private conversation. Mum and Dad should know that and not spill their tea all over the kitchen table where anyone can hear...ewww...anyway..." Clem tried to continue, but let out a muffled shriek instead and started to sob.

Daisy and Royce looked at each other in amusement. "Did you touch the spider webs, Clem?"

"Yes!"

"Is Dad at work?"

"Yes."

"And where is Mum?"

"She's inside having a lie down."

"Clem, listen to me," said Royce, taking the phone from Daisy. "I think you can probably go outside and talk from there. You might wake Mum up if you keep screeching like that," he continued, winking at Daisy.

"Oh yeah, good point. Hang on."

Daisy and Royce listened to the sounds of Clem scrambling out of the shed. It was a Halloween horror of a shed. She had refused to step foot in there for at least six years now. She gave Clem props for braving it in the name of family discretion.

"Ok, I'm out and I'm ok."

"What's going on Clementine, what is worrying you?" asked Royce, concern filling his voice again. He loved his little sister dearly, even if she was quite hair-brained sometimes.

"Ok you guys, you know how Mum hasn't been working for a bit? Well, apparently, they have missed a few payments, and the bank is getting cranky with them."

"Oh shit!" Daisy looked up at Royce in alarm. "Did you overhear all of this?"

"No, as soon I realised what was going on, I went in and demanded they tell me everything. They said everything was fine, and that they had it under control, but basically, they need eighteen thousand dollars in time for their next mortgage payment."

"I don't understand. We've been helping them out with money. How are they so far behind?" asked Royce.

"They were pretty sketchy about it, but apparently,

they have had a backdated debt for a while and the bank is getting nasty and wants them to repay it more quickly."

"When is the next payment due?" asked Daisy, a familiar feeling of guilt sitting heavy in her belly. This was her fault.

"They pay quarterly, so I think they have another two months left. They said they would be able to find the money, but they made me swear I wouldn't tell you guys because they don't want to worry you."

"They are such bloody maniacs! No, you did the right thing, Clem. Thanks for letting us know."

Royce looked down at Daisy, his face worried. "Yeah, thanks Clemmie. Listen, we will find the money ok. No one is getting kicked out of the house."

"Love you Clem!"

Later, after Royce had filled Arabella in on the news from home, the three of them sat out on the balcony, trying to find a way out of the family's problems.

"We can always sell the apartment," said Arabella quietly.

"Yeah, that was what I was thinking," replied Royce tiredly.

Daisy looked around at them in alarm. "No way. Look, we will figure this out. I can get the sale bought forward. We will make it work. No one is selling their house, ok!"

———

Determined to make some much-needed cash for the baby and for his parents, Royce had jetted off to the Pacific this time, to cover a political meeting attended by Australia's

Foreign Minister. This left Daisy to be Arabella's date at a few of her more high-profile work events.

Later that afternoon, after a swim and a smoothie, Daisy was sitting at the kitchen table, working on the shop's tax return, when she got a text from Arabella.

Fancy a fancy night out? Put on something glam and meet me at the Opera Bar. Launch party for a new TV show! Be there at 6!

I guess it is Friday, Daisy reasoned, slamming shut her laptop and texting a quick rsvp back to Arabella.

After a quick shower, she stood in front of the mirror, assessing a white baby-doll lace dress she had made a few weeks ago. The dress had three-quarter sleeves and a skirt which draped softly to her knees. It was part of her new experimental range, and she was quite proud of how well it had turned out. This was the first chance she'd had to wear it and she was excited to dress it up. Daisy quickly twisted her wavy hair up into a messy bun and added her favourite gold spiral studs. Something was missing though, and she tilted her head to the side for a moment, contemplating her small suitcase of choices.

Suddenly a wicked thought crossed her mind, and she dashed across the hall into Arabella and Royce's room, flinging open Arabella's wardrobe as she greeted its contents exuberantly.

"Hello darlings!"

There, stretched across the back wall of the walk in, was a shoe lover's heaven, rack after rack of expensive and beautiful shoes, in all shapes and styles and colours. While Arabella typically spent most of her income reinvesting in her business, she allowed herself one weakness—shoes.

Luckily, she didn't need to spend too much, as the designers and stylists she knew through work were more than happy to gift her a pair in exchange for a favour or two. Best of all, Arabella was always happy to share with her sisters and best friends if they were ever in need of the perfect shoe. In fact, Arabella had become known within the family as a bit of a shoe librarian, express posting many a pair to Byron and Brisbane over the years. Daisy looked over the racks until she settled on one pair in particular. Grinning in delight, she scooped them up off the shelf and danced back to her room.

Daisy slipped on the shoes and gazed at her reflection in the mirror. The heels glinted like liquid gold in the afternoon sunlight, giving a structured, industrial edge to the otherwise whimsical dress. Daisy slid on an almost identical molten gold bangle and slung her go-to brown satchel bag over her shoulder.

Yep, not bad at all! she thought appraisingly.

———

An hour later, Daisy met Arabella at the top of the stairs of the Sydney Opera House forecourt. Daisy smiled at the sight of her best friend, standing in front of the majestic white sails of the iconic building, looking immaculate in her trademark pencil legged trousers, a sleeveless trench coat dress and towering stilettos. Oversized black sunglasses and her ice blonde bob and blunt fringe, sitting perfectly despite the warm afternoon, completed her look. She had headphones in and was speaking on the phone a mile a minute while simultaneously typing an email.

"Thanks for coming, lovely!" Arabella said, hugging her, still on the phone. "You look great...especially in my shoes!"

Daisy laughed. "You won't be able to wear these for much longer and someone will need to keep them company! I'm just getting to know my new friends!"

It was good hanging out with Arabella again. In fact, it was almost as if no time had passed at all, and the two girls had easily slipped back into their old friendship.

After Arabella finished her call, they walked down the stairs to the Opera Bar.

"So this is the launch of the new show, *Lost at Sea*. It's kind of a Swiss Family Robinson theme, only instead of it being a family of castaways, it's competing houses of reality tv stars. And there are multiple families," she explained.

"So, like Survivor meets Big Brother?" asked Daisy.

"Exactly! Only each Robinson Family house is a Big Brother house, and they are competing against each other AND against the other families."

"Surely this has been done a million times before?" laughed Daisy, with a bewildered shake of her head.

Arabella laughed. "Yes, but we never say that out loud. What we say out loud is that it's a genius idea!"

A distinguished-looking man in his fifties was walking past as Arabella made her proclamation.

"Arabella, good to see you! It is a genius idea; I was just saying that to Arkie and Shola!"

The man, clearly a marketing executive from the tv network, air kissed in Arabella's general direction before walking ahead of them.

Arabella and Daisy looked at each other and stifled giggles.

"So why are you here?" Daisy asked.

"My company represents one of the hosts. She's a real media pro, so this is really a junket for me, and I thought it would be a good place for you to be seen. Plus, there is this Home and Away star I am dying to get my hands on..."

Daisy stopped and turned at her best friend's lascivious tone.

"Really?" she laughed, rolling her eyes.

"No, of course not. I'm kidding! He's a hot soapie star who is about to become very famous. And I want to work with his agent. Come on, I'll point him out if he is here!"

As they reached the lower mezzanine, Daisy's eyes widened. The main seating area outside the bar had been roped off and turned into an actual tropical island. A large wooden sailing boat was jutting out of a faux sandy beach. Palm trees swayed in the strategically piped in summer breeze, scented, of course, with the sweet fragrance of coconut and pineapple. A volcano towered above the ship, rumbling ominously now and then, while a waterfall cascaded cool turquoise water down onto the beach. Daisy's jaw dropped as she took in the opulent set design, before she realised that all the people inside the roped off area were, in fact, some of Australia's most famous celebrities. Cameras flashed as Daisy and Arabella posed on the red carpet before being ushered through security and into the tropical bower inside. Someone thrust a glass of champagne in her hand and Daisy gazed around in awe. Soapie stars and movie stars mingled with television talent show winners and famous sports players. Child star turned disco queen

Kia Brownlow was talking to Lee Seb, winner of last year's Australia's Got Pop. Academy Award winner Alba Andrews was standing next to the country's most infamous television presenter, Mike Sokolov and two winners from previous seasons of Put a Ring on It. Australia's number one ranked tennis player Jax Turpin and his supermodel girlfriend Nan Sinclair were taking selfies next to the talking robot parrot. It was a ridiculous explosion of celebrity and Daisy stood in the middle of the party, entranced as the famous revellers surged around her.

A tall, blonde woman wearing a skintight red dress, leopard print stilettos and a matching leopard print cape strode over to where Arabella and Daisy were standing. Her lips were so plump and her boobs so perfectly round and perky that Daisy was certain neither could be real.

"Arabella, darling! So good to see you!" The tall woman spoke with a mix of drag queen husk and languid privilege. Daisy gulped down a snort of laughter at the juxtaposition, mesmerized by the woman's cleavage, which stayed perfectly still despite her many flamboyant hand gestures. "What a turnout! Prudencia will be wildly happy."

"She will!" replied Arabella enthusiastically, switching into work mode. "Lozza darling, I'd like you to meet Daisy Gardiner. Daisy is a fashion designer from the North Coast in town for the Sydney Fashion Festival. Daisy, please meet one of my absolute favourite clients, Lozza Rothermere-Smythe, breakout star of the tv show Sydney Confidential."

They paused for a moment to have their photo taken before resuming their conversation.

"Oh the north coast is divine, Roban and I are always talking about buying a little beach shack up north, just something simple for us to get away to - the Palm Beach house is just too exposed these days...how clever of you to get on to that trend and get established before the Sydney hordes start descending...well we all say we are ready to get out of this town, I mean the property prices alone are horrendous, we are always trying to get out of Rose Bay and get up into Vaucluse...who can live in a house with just 5 bedrooms! I tell you..."

Arabella winked discreetly at Daisy, who had tuned out of Lozza's monologue and was again looking around at all the beautiful people, laughing and smiling and having their photos taken incessantly. If they weren't posing for a photographer, they were busy taking selfies. It was a strange and intoxicating party and Daisy wasn't sure what to do with herself.

Suddenly, a hushed murmur rippled through the gaggle of celebrities. The crowd parted and a tall man, with piercing blue eyes and the tightest white t-shirt Daisy had ever seen on a person, began striding towards them. His sandy blonde hair fell casually across his tanned forehead, tousled gently as though he had just gotten out of bed. He was wearing well-fitting black jeans and a lightweight navy cardigan, and white sneakers. He strode through the crowd with just the right amount of arrogant swagger, seemingly oblivious to the famous faces around him. The overall effect was, smooth, casual and glamourous.

And 100% fucking drop-dead sexy.

Bloody hell! thought Daisy in disbelief as she watched him move through the crowds. *It's like Zac Efron and Chris Hemsworth had a baby. And that baby grew up to have a baby with Ryan Gosling. No human should ever be allowed to look that good in real life!*

It was true, this man made all the other celebrities at the party look pale and insignificant, no easy feat given the over-abundance of beautiful people surrounding them. Daisy continued to gape as the man continued to stride through the crowd. She tilted her head to one side and wondered if he was moving in slow motion for everyone or if that was just her?

Suddenly she realised he was still walking directly towards her, and she looked around nervously, trying to figure out why he was looking straight at her, and walking so purposefully in her direction.

Why is he coming over here? Is he coming over here to talk to me? What will I say to him? I can't talk to him! I can't even breathe! Oh shit! How do I breathe again?

By this time, the man was standing a mere 20 centimetres from Daisy, so close she could smell him. *Oh God, he probably smells that good naturally,* she thought, unwillingly imagining what it would feel like to reach out and trace the outline of his very well-defined six-pack. Her fingers twitched, and she shoved her hands into her pockets in a panic. *Get a grip Gardiner! That would not be cool!*

"Arabella!" he said, holding out his arms and pushing Daisy to the side in one fluid motion. "There's my favourite PR queen!"

Daisy stumbled to the side as he leant forward and kissed Arabella theatrically, while every woman within a five-metre radius turned green with envy, shivering in delight as they imaged what it would be like to kiss those famous, luscious lips.

"Mack, good to see you," said Arabella, firmly pushing the handsome man off her and taking a step back, putting a little bit of distance between them. Cameras followed Mack wherever he went and as a savvy PR manager, Arabella knew she wasn't the story. Daisy was, however, and she discreetly reached out and pulled Daisy back into the circle, strategically positioning her so that she would be in every frame with Mack.

"Daisy, I'd like you to meet Mack Boddington—you might recognise him from Home and Away—Mack is currently negotiating a couple of big Hollywood films. I provide some additional support to Mack's agent from time to time." Arabella raised her eyebrows almost imperceptibly at Daisy.

"Mack, I'd like you to meet Daisy Gardiner, fashion designer and owner of the label Garden and Bay." Arabella saw the disinterest in the tv stars eyes and quickly added "... and my sister-in-law."

Mack acknowledged Arabella's introduction with a bow and turned to Daisy. For a minute he stood and stared at her, his expression completely unreadable, before he took her hand and kissed it gently. Daisy gulped. It was as if a thousand small horses had run the Melbourne Cup in her knickers, and she never wanted them to stop.

"Well hello Daisy Gardiner," he said suggestively, his eyes locked on her and only her.

For a second Daisy felt the rest of the world float away as she stared up into those bright blue eyes.

All she could muster in reply was a very un-cool 'Hey'.

"How are the contract negotiations going?" Arabella

asked, shaking her head affectionately at her star-struck friend and turning back to Mack.

"Contracts are so boring Arabella...I wish you would come and sort all that out for me. Brian doesn't do it anywhere near as well as you!" Mack let go of Daisy's hand and turned back to Arabella. Daisy took in a big gulp of air and tried to remember how to stand up straight.

"Brian is the best agent in Australia, and you are lucky to have him!" replied Arabella, scolding the star gently, while managing to hide a triumphant grin. She paused for a minute, as though she was mulling over her schedule. "But you know, I've got a bit of time free at the moment, now that Nan's skincare line has launched...I could definitely be persuaded to come on-board as a consultant to support Brian."

They chatted for a bit before Mack wandered off to greet some of the other beautiful people at the party. As he turned to leave, he looked Daisy over again, his expression a mixture of boredom and disdain, and something else Daisy couldn't quite read. It was unsettling.

Once Mack was out of earshot, Arabella turned to Daisy.

"You ok?" she asked, smiling at a very flushed Daisy.

"Uh-huh...next time give me a bit of warning that might happen!" laughed Daisy, still annoyingly a little breathless.

Arabella leaned forward to quietly fill Daisy in on Mack's backstory.

"Don't be deceived by his exquisite exterior. That man is serious trouble. He is a great talent and destined to go far. If only he can keep his pants, and his dealer's baggie, zipped up long enough to get some work done. He is so bloody conceited. Well, who wouldn't be when you look like that, and he sleeps with pretty much everyone he meets. He is meant to be keeping a low profile as Brian negotiates two very exciting movie deals—Wes Anderson and Michael Bay."

Arabella looked at Daisy, who was still a little flustered, and sighed.

"Seriously, don't be fooled by his charm—he is a dreadful man. I've seen way too many young wannabes get sucked up into his orbit. And I wouldn't be doing business with him except for the fact he is very talented and about to be very famous."

As Arabella talked, Daisy's eyes followed Mack around the party. He was startlingly good looking, with a serious dash of mischief twinkling in his obscenely blue eyes. But he also seemed spoilt and wilful, sending back drinks, slapping bottoms and rubbing himself up against a certain well-known male newsreader.

Daisy looked back at Arabella and exhaled, happy to have regained a little of her composure.

"Oh my gosh, that was wild! He is so good-looking," laughed Daisy, a little self-consciously. "He's not my type at all, but wow!"

Arabella smiled knowingly and shook her head. "Are you going to be ok if I leave you for a few minutes? I am just going to do the rounds, and then we can find a quiet table and watch the chaos unfold."

"I'll be fine. I'll stay right here, I promise!"

After Arabella disappeared into the crowd, Daisy scanned the party, hoping to flag down a waiter and nab another glass of champagne. She watched, fascinated, as the assembled guests all seemed to be drawn to Mack Boddington, who was more than happy to be the centre of attention.

And yet every time he looked up, he seemed to look right at her, his expression dark and his eyebrows raised, just a fraction, in acknowledgement.

And every time Daisy shivered slightly at the feel of his eyes on her.

Is he really looking at me? Good God, I need another drink!

Finally, Daisy caught the attention of one of the wait staff, who smiled knowingly in Mack's direction as he walked over to where Daisy was standing.

"He's illegally handsome, isn't he," the waiter said, as he leant in to offer Daisy the last glass of bubbles from his tray.

Daisy blushed. "Oh no, was I being that obvious?"

The waiter laughed. "Don't worry, I've seen worse. Besides, people that beautiful should come with a warning label."

Daisy looked up to find Mack in the crowd again. He had taken a few steps closer to where she was standing, but now had his arms around a young tv starlet and was pressing his lips suggestively into her neck.

A wave of disappointment washed through Daisy.

See Daisy, he wasn't looking at you. You were just imagining it.

"Sure, he might be pretty, but I mean, look at him. He doesn't look all that smart, does he?" she replied, more spitefully than she meant to. "I don't think he is the sharpest tool in the shed."

"Ooh, burn! You are nasty, girl! I love it! I am going to bring you some more champagne!"

As the waiter left to refill his tray, Arabella made her way back over to Daisy.

"Hey babe, would you be disappointed if we head home early? My work is done, and my feet are killing me. We could get some takeaway and watch some Netflix?"

Daisy looked at her in relief. "Oh my God, I am so glad you said that! Yes! Let's get out of here!

Still, as Arabella and Daisy walked through the crowd, Daisy couldn't help but look over to where Mack was standing, now just a few metres from them. She caught his eye, and he looked back at her, glaring and defiant now, as if he had just heard everything she had said to the waiter a few moments before. He languidly and deliberately trailed his gaze up and down her body and winked suggestively. She shivered, unsure if she felt horrified or turned on by his leering.

Suddenly, he turned and leapt agilely up onto the bow of the pirate ship. "Excuse me folks, just gotta take a leak. Where's the chamber pot on this old rust bucket then?" he slurred, unzipping his jeans to the gasps of everyone at the party - horror from those in the crowd below him, and potentially in the splash zone, and delight from the assembled paparazzi, who were holding their collective breath waiting for the shot of the century.

"Oh, good grief," groaned Arabella, thrusting her bag at Daisy and pushing her way through the crowd to her delinquent almost-client. But Mack saw her coming and decided to stage dive off the ship and into the crowd, his pants slipping down around his knees as he landed on Lozza Rothermere-Smythe and Trina Truesdale, a chirpy breakfast tv host.

The crowd erupted into chaos as Mack reached out to squeeze one of Lozza's unmoving breasts.

"Why hello there, ladies. It seems I've fallen for you both rather hard. Fancy taking this party back to my hotel room?"

———

Daisy tumbled out of bed the next morning to meet Dan for their regular surf. She'd had far too many glasses of champagne at the Lost at Sea party last night. After Mack's crowd surfing incident, Arabella had dashed off to help Brian with damage control, leaving Daisy with nothing to do but keep drinking the very expensive and very free champagne. She'd found a nice table, tucked away from the melee, and set up camp to wait for Arabella.

After her first few glasses, her waiter friend had discreetly brought her over a bottle and an ice bucket and a plate of sashimi. Daisy spent the next hour sipping bubbly and watching the celebrities and paparazzi go into meltdown as Mack left a trail of anarchy in his wake.

When she got down to the beach the following morning, she was secretly relieved to see that the sea was flat. Instead, Dan was waiting for her on the sea wall stairs, coffee in one hand and a bacon and egg roll in the other.

"Dan, you have no idea how much I need this right now!"

"Yeah, I think I do...have you turned on your phone this morning?

Daisy shook her head as she took a bite of the hot, salty breakfast burger.

Dan pulled out his phone and opened up the Sydney Morning Herald website.

"Looks like you made front page news," he said with a wry grin, showing her a series of photos of Mack Boddington kissing her hand and standing next to her. The angle of the photographs made it look like they were sharing an intimate moment, with no one else around them, and there was something about the way Mack was looking down at Daisy that seemed so private and gentle.

Daisy groaned and dropped her head into her palms as she remembered the way he looked at her from across the party. Arabella was right, Mack Boddington was trouble.

"Do you know this guy for real?" Dan continued, sounding a little more annoyed now.

"Not at all!" she said, lifting her head up to explain. "Actually, I can't believe how that photo was set up! Arabella was right beside me and I was just introduced to him that second. Anyway, he is such a dick...later in the night he got super drunk and decided he would pee off the side of this giant boat that was part of the party decorations. And then he jumped into the crowd and started dry humping one of the housewives from Sydney Confidential. It was ridiculous!"

Daisy stopped and shook her head, trying to get the memory of those piercing blue eyes out of her mind. "Why am I still talking about that idiot?" she laughed. "He doesn't deserve any more publicity than he already has!"

"I made my dress, though," she continued shyly. "What do you think?"

"No way! You made that? It looks really great. I mean, you looked really great." Dan looked down at Daisy and took a deep breath. "You looked beautiful, actually," he said with a gentle smile.

Jumping up, Dan reached out his hand to Daisy. "Come on, since we can't surf today, I have something I want to show you."

Daisy followed Dan along Hall Street, past the Vinnies op-shop and down several side streets, into one she'd never noticed before. Forest Knoll Avenue was a short, dead-end street, but it was lined with several beautiful, large leafy trees and every house seemed to have a well looked after fence and a colourful garden.

"My family has owned this house since my grandparents first married in 1943," Dan explained, as he opened the gate to the cottage at the end of the street. It was a white weatherboard with navy trim—Daisy thought it looked very cute.

Inside the house, it was lighter than she expected, thanks to the wall of bi-fold doors running across the entire back wall. The doors opened out onto a large, partially covered deck, which looked out over the most beautiful garden Daisy had ever seen.

Daisy and Dan walked out on the deck and stood up against the railing, gazing out into the backyard.

"Dan, did you do this?" Daisy asked, looking at the wild sea of green below. It was a secret, magic place. A large flame tree grew in one corner, while smaller palm trees and ferns vied for space amongst monstrous-sized monstera, a banana tree and a stand of bamboo. Frangipanis, bird of paradise and hibiscus, competed for the title of the most glorious flower, while the sweet scent of jasmine hung thickly in the air.

"It reminds me of home!" she said, feeling herself relax into the little tropical oasis.

Daisy looked up at Dan, who was smiling proudly.

"I started looking after the garden when I was thirteen, helping my grandmother maintain it when it became too hard for her to do it. We worked out the plans together—she always wanted a tropical garden—she grew up in Papua New Guinea, so she always wanted something to remind her of home, as she called it. I mean, she lived here for 64 years, but it was still home." Dan chuckled affectionately at the memory of his grandmother.

Dan and Daisy took a seat on the stairs leading down to the small grassy area before the rainforest started. Costello had curled up in a nice sunny spot and was snoring loudly.

"My mother died when I was very young, and my father couldn't cope with a toddler, so he dropped me off here at my Grandparent's house. Alice and Ron. They were my mother's parents."

Daisy reached out to hold Dan's hand because it seemed like the right thing to do.

"So I grew up here on this street, playing in this garden, all of my life."

"Grandpa Ron died when I was in high school and then my grandma after I had finished uni. I wasn't living here then. I'd moved away to Wollongong to study, but I came back when she got sick and stayed looking after her. We were almost done in the garden, but she died before it was completely finished, so I kept going. I inherited the house and this lazy dog. So here I am."

"Dan, this garden is amazing! I am sure your grandma loved it...and loved knowing what it was going to grow into!"

"I like to think so," replied Dan, looking around his backyard with pride. "And you know, it's not a sad story, really. Although it sucks, I never knew my mum or dad and it was sad losing Ron and Alice. They were both really awesome. But I've had an amazing life here. And hey, I own a house in Bondi! That's pretty unheard of for someone our age! I mean, I'm no Bondi super-model, or Mack Bodding-ton, but I think I'm doing ok."

Daisy turned to face the sweet and handsome man beside her. "You are amazing, Dan!"

Impulsively, Daisy leant forward and kissed him, softly. He didn't respond and Daisy pulled back, her cheeks flushed with embarrassment.

"Oh, I am so sorry, I totally misread that..."

Her words were stopped as Dan reached out and pulled her close, kissing her back this time, a long lingering kiss that took Daisy's breath away. They kissed for what seemed like an age, tasting the salt from the sea breeze on each other's lips, getting lost in the warmth of each other. Dan reached his hand up and tangled it in Daisy's hair, while Daisy let her hands wander up Dan's chest and around his neck. She loved she could feel his heart beating fast as she pressed herself deeper into his arms.

"I've wanted to do that since the first moment I saw you," confessed Dan, a little sheepishly.

"Oh me too!" laughed Daisy. "I'm so glad it wasn't just me!"

"It was definitely not just you," replied Dan, pulling her even closer towards him so he could kiss the side of her neck.

They sat for a while in the sunshine, their hands entwined, and huge grins plastered across both of their faces.

Finally, Daisy broke the silence and pulled away.

"So...um, I have to tell you something," she said, looking down at the ground, the familiar waves of fear rising in her belly. She pushed them away and took a deep breath.

"When I was 18, my high school boyfriend left me at a party, and I had to call my mum to come and get me in the middle of the night. It had been raining, and we had a car accident on the way home. Luckily, no one else was involved. But Mum and I were pretty badly hurt, and I had to have a few operations. My parents had to go into debt to pay for all my hospital bills. And Jordan and I broke up pretty soon after that."

Daisy paused for a bit. It was not that what she was about to tell him was bad, it was just that the very few times she had told other guys she had been interested in, this was the moment they ended things.

"It took a long time for me to recover, and I haven't really had a proper boyfriend since, so I'm a bit nervous about all this..."

Dan moved up a step and pulled Daisy in between his legs, so that she was leaning up against his chest. He nuzzled into her hair and kissed the top of her head.

"That sounds really awful Daisy," he said. "But trust me, it's just like riding a bike. You'll see."

That wasn't what Daisy meant, and she considered interrupting him, but Dan had started kissing the other side of her neck in a way that was making goosebumps bubble up and down her arms and legs. It wasn't the right time. Perhaps she would tell him later.

"I really like you Daisy Gardiner...and I really want to keep getting to know you!"

Daisy smiled and relaxed. Despite her misgivings, for the first time in a very long time, she wondered if perhaps she might just get a shot at romance after all.

Six

SydneyShhh! *Find out who made the VIP list to get 'Lost at Sea' and see our exclusive photos of Home and Away hottie Mack Boddington's wild night out! Click through for all the raunchy, behind-the-scenes adventures!*

———

"Bloody hell, isn't it just my luck that I score the biggest client of my life and I can't even have a bloody glass of champagne to celebrate!"

Arabella, Royce, Daisy, and Dan were sitting out on the veranda of Royce and Arabella's apartment, celebrating Arabella's freshly minted contract with Mack Boddington. After the fiasco at the Lost at Sea party, Mack's agent had called Arabella, begging for her help, keeping Mack's public image on track until his two big contracts were signed.

Arabella eyed off the glass of sparkling apple juice her husband had poured for her and grimaced.

"The things we sacrifice for our children," she sighed

dramatically, causing Daisy and Dan to laugh out loud and Royce to shake his head in mock despair.

The four of them were celebrating Arabella's news with dinner on the balcony, enjoying the warm, late summer weather. A balmy breeze fluttered the strands of fairy lights, softly casting small shadows over the table. The languid, bluesy twangs of Howlin' Wolf floated out of the speakers and out onto the breeze.

Daisy and Dan had been pretty much inseparable since last Saturday morning, when they had first kissed in Dan's backyard. Royce and Arabella both thought it was great that Daisy had finally given in to a summer fling and had invited Dan around so they could get to know him better.

Royce had met Dan a few times over the last few days. Dan had initially been a little star-struck meeting Royce for the first time. He later told Daisy that 'Love you too', Mulligan's Mercy's most famous single, was the first song he had learnt to play on guitar and that he had seen the band play at least four times when he was a teenager. But the initial awkwardness had soon passed when the two men had struck a friendship over Royce's home brews and a shared love of landscape photography. Arabella was a little more reserved, having only just met him, and she was watching them quietly as they sat around the table on the balcony.

"So, AB, tell me, what is Mack Boddington really like? After I saw those photos of him and Daisy at the Opera Bar, I thought I had no chance with her," joked Dan as he grinned and squeezed Daisy's hand.

Arabella snorted into her apple juice. "Oh love, you've got nothing to worry about there! This guy is an absolute horror and Daisy has much better taste than that! And he mostly prefers the company of vacuous young models, anyway. That is when he is not enjoying the company of any illicit substance he can get his hands on. His proclivities - both sexual and narcotic - will be the death of him and his career!"

Daisy laughed. "Now, now, Arabella, no talking trash about your clients, remember!" she teased.

Arabella looked around the table for a second before shaking her head. "Oh dear! Of course, this is all totally off the record, right? I'm being incredibly indiscreet! Just between us! Promise?"

The others laughed and promised to keep her celebrity secrets.

Dan looked across at Daisy and smiled.

"I have nothing to worry about then? You aren't going to run off with him? Not sure I could compete with a stud like that," Daisy was sure Dan was joking, but she could see Arabella's eyebrows raise just slightly, as she turned to reply.

"No way! Guys like that do not excite me at all. I told you, he wouldn't even remember me, anyway."

Dan smiled. "I'm just glad that your little experiment with the celebrity set is nearly over."

"Oh really?" asked Arabella, as she and Royce looked at Daisy in surprise.

"Yes, I talked it over with Dan and we decided I will make my decision by the start of the Fashion Festival. It will be good to get a decision made and start moving on with my life."

"Don't you think you should wait until the end of

Fashion Fest though, Daisy? I mean, there is lots to see and learn that may impact your decision," said Royce.

"Yeah, but I don't see why Daisy needs to do that when she has you guys. I mean, you both work in the fashion and media industry and can tell her everything she needs, right?"

"Yes, exactly! I don't really need to spend too much time on these things when I have you guys!"

Arabella glanced at Royce, a brief look of alarm flickering across her face. But Royce was too busy topping up the wine glasses to notice.

"Ok, well, it's your decision Daisy," Arabella said, turning back to the table.

Changing the subject, Royce stood up and raised his glass to Arabella.

"I think my very awesome and clever wife deserves a toast...AB, you are amazing, and this is so incredibly well deserved. I don't know anyone who works harder than you or deserves this kind of success more. Congratulations darling!"

Talk around the table turned to other, more exciting things. Royce was heading back to Fiji in a few months for another diplomatic event and he and Arabella were planning a quick holiday at the end, to spend some time together before the baby came.

Daisy watched her brother and best friend affectionately as they spoke animatedly of their trip together and what they were planning to do. She remembered how much they used to argue as kids and how their friendship blossomed into love.

I hope one day someone looks at me the way these two look

at each other, she thought, shyly looking up at Dan, and feeling her heart quicken as he laughed at something Arabella said, his eyes crinkling in the way that Daisy loved.

Across the table, Arabella watched Daisy and Dan with growing apprehension. For the first time in ages, Daisy was falling for someone. But from everything she'd seen that night, Arabella wasn't sure Daisy was falling for the right person.

———

Later that night, after Dan had left and Royce was busy in the kitchen, Arabella looked across at Daisy, appraisingly,

"So, Dan seems like an interesting guy," she said casually.

"He is so sweet, isn't he," Daisy replied, staring dreamily out into the night sky, oblivious to Arabella's tone.

"Yeah, he seems really sweet. He seems a bit insecure too, though, don't you think?"

Daisy's attention was brought back to the table. "What do you mean?"

"Well, he's really fixated on you and Mack, even though you only met that one time. Plus, he seems to be pretty sure about what you should do with Garden and Bay."

"What are you trying to say Arabella?" Daisy asked, suddenly feeling a little wary. She knew Arabella too well to know these were idle questions.

"Oh, I don't know, just, don't be too apologetic. You haven't done anything wrong. And this is your life, you know. This is your decision to make."

Daisy thought back to some of the conversations she'd

had with Dan about her shop and why she was here in Sydney. It did make her uncomfortable sometimes, when he was pushy about his opinion. But he was so sweet most of the time and cute, and she was having such a good time hanging out with him. She decided to ignore those feelings for a while and just enjoy the moment.

"Arabella, I don't know what you are talking about. Dan is lovely and everything is fine!"

Arabella sighed, knowing that she was getting nowhere with this conversation.

"Sorry babe. I guess I just want everything to be good for you. This is an exciting time for all of us. Let's go help Royce in the kitchen."

———

Arabella's celebrations didn't last long. After a few overcast days, Bondi was back to its usual, sparkling, sunny self. Daisy and Dan were at Ravesi's pub with Louie and Fern, enjoying a few drinks and some sunbathing when Arabella called her.

"Oh, sorry you guys, this is Arabella. I should take it," said Daisy, standing up and moving to the edge of the veranda.

"Hey girlfriend, what's up?" she said.

"Daiz, I can't talk long. I've just snuck out of a meeting to use the loo."

Daisy smiled in amusement and stage whispered into the phone.

"AB? Why are you whispering?"

"I told you, I'm in the loo!"

"I don't think that explains it," replied Daisy drily.

"I'm hiding from Mack, and I can't talk in case someone else is in here. Wait, let me check."

Daisy could hear some doors rattling and banging and waited patiently for Arabella's sleuthing to conclude.

"Ok," Arabella said brightly and at usual volume. "We are alone!"

"AB, what is going on?" laughed Daisy.

Arabella sighed. "I knew he was an idiot," she said. "I just didn't realize he was this bad!"

"What's he done now?" Daisy asked, more to support Arabella than for any interest in the odious Mack Boddington.

"Well, you know how Mack is negotiating a contract with Wes Anderson? Well, Wes' contract lawyer and assistant, who just happens to be his niece, are here in Sydney and we were about to sign when we noticed that Mack and the niece were missing - we found them shagging in Brian's photo-copier room. The contract lawyer immediately called Wes, who got angry and retracted 50 percent of the salary we had just finished negotiating..."

On the other end of the line, a door creaked open, and Daisy heard a man's voice call out.

"Arabella? Where are you? Are you in here? Did you see Brian's face when he saw me getting stuck into it with that girl? Hilarious!"

"Shit, it's him - ugh, he's just so dumb!" Arabella hissed, before abruptly changing tone. "Darling fab news, thanks for sharing, will talk more about this when I get home later, bye!"

Daisy looked down at her phone, shaking her head. She

didn't envy Arabella her job at all, and she wondered if it was always like this in the fashion and media world. From what she'd seen so far, Royce was right, it wasn't the nicest field to work in, even if it was exciting and full of so many beautiful people.

Daisy re-joined the table.

"Was that AB?" asked Dan.

"Yeah, sorry, she is having trouble with one of her clients. I think she just needed a quick vent."

"Was it Mack?"

Daisy looked at Dan carefully.

"I don't know," she replied vaguely. "She didn't say."

"I bet it was him. He is such a jerk." Dan stood up quickly, noisily scraping his chair as he rose. "I'm getting another jug. Same again ok?"

The rest of the table nodded in agreement. Daisy felt uncomfortable, as though she had done something wrong, so she smiled and followed Dan inside.

———

Later that night, Daisy was out on the balcony, bringing her washing in and getting her swimmers and towel ready for her now regular early morning surf or swim with Dan. Arabella was at a work event until late and Royce was in the study, packing his camera gear ready for his latest trip away, just to Tasmania this time, so she was surprised to hear the front door slam and a loud clatter come from the kitchen. Daisy quickly stepped back in from the balcony, just in time to see Arabella staggering into the lounge, too exhausted to even make a joke at her own expense. Daisy watched in alarm as she sat down on the couch and closed her eyes, breathing deeply as if waiting for the world to stop spinning.

"AB, are you ok?" she asked, walking over to best friend. "Royce, get in here!"

Arabella looked up at Daisy, her eyes tired and red. She nodded but before she could say anything, she burst into tears. Royce walked in and immediately dashed over to the lounge.

"AB! What's wrong? Are you ok? Is the baby ok?"

"I'm fine, you guys, really. Just exhausted and I've been sick all day," she said, in between sobs. "It's been hard hiding the morning sickness and managing Mack's contract negotiations."

She wearily shook her head. "It's hard just managing Mack."

Arabella looked up at her best friend and her husband, who were both looking at her with identical expressions of concern. They looked so much alike at times and shared so many of the same expressions. She smiled at them affectionately, as she wiped away her tears.

"Daisy, could you please make me some vegemite toast?" she asked hopefully.

"Of course!" Daisy jumped up and moved into the kitchen to make the toast.

Royce sat on the lounge next to AB and wrapped his arms around her.

"Do you want me to cancel the trip?" he asked, worriedly. "I should stay home and look after you more."

"No babe, it's fine, really, I'm just tired—it's nothing a bit of sleep and a lot of food won't fix. Besides, this contract negotiation will be over soon, and things will go back to normal, and my pregnancy contingency plan will kick in." Arabella looked up gratefully as Daisy brought over the toast. She closed her eyes as she took a bite, savoring the buttery, salty snack.

"I really hate that you have to be in this situation with Mack. He's such a jerk," frowned Royce.

"I know, but it's a pretty big make or break moment for the company. If we can get him through the next week, then we will have really cemented our reputation as crisis managers in the field. Usually, I love this work! It's just hard when I'm not feeling well and when I'm so tired."

Arabella looked at Daisy and Royce, willing them to understand.

"I know Mack is a jerk, but it's my job to protect his reputation, and I'm really good at this. So, you know how he is on the verge of scoring two big roles, one with Wes Anderson, where he will be working with Bill Murray and Cate Blanchett? Well, the other role is even bigger—the lead in Michael Bay's remake of He-Man. That's going to be the next blockbuster, trust me! And Hollywood is still pretty conservative and both roles are his as long as he can keep it together long enough to get through both film shoots. But we all know Mack is in the midst of a long-standing chemical romance and his penchant for sex with anyone and anything that moves means my number one priority is to keep him out of trouble."

They all sat quietly for a moment, digesting Arabella's words.

"AB, I know you are the best in the business," Royce said carefully, stroking Arabella's hand gently. "But this is really stressful for you and the baby. Don't you think it's kind of more like you are babysitting, rather than managing a PR campaign?"

Arabella bristled and pulled away from her husband. "I would never make assumptions about your work, Royce! How dare you presume to know about mine! You don't know what my job actually entails, and whether this client is any different!"

Daisy looked down as her brother and best friend descended into yet another argument and discreetly slipped out of the room and into her bedroom. But it was no good. Even with her door shut, she could hear them clearly.

"I am so sick of this baby already," Arabella said. "You wanted this baby more than me. I don't want to do this anymore!"

"That is not true Arabella, and you know it! It was your idea!"

"Because you wanted a baby! You are such a great guy, Royce. I wanted to be able to give you what you wanted."

Arabella and Royce fell silent for a moment.

"I don't like what this is doing to me, Royce," Arabella finally said. "This baby is already making me so tired and sick...what is it going to be like when it comes? It's already the end of my career and I want to do something big, just once before I have to give it all up!"

"You won't have to give it up Arabella, we've already talked about this. I want to stay home with you and the baby and I am perfectly happy to be as much of a stay at-home parent as you need."

"But what will your mum say? Won't she think I'm a bad mum?"

"My mother would kick my arse if she thought for a second I was going to let you be a stay-at-home mum, you know that!"

Daisy felt bad, as though she was intruding on a very private moment. She picked up her phone and sent a quick text. As soon as she got a reply, she flew around the room, throwing a few bits and pieces into an overnight bag. Once she was packed, she scribbled a few words on a note, which she stuck to Royce and Arabella's bedroom door.

Gone to Dan's for the night. See you tomorrow, love you xx, the note read.

———

Dan was waiting for her on the front porch. He had obviously just had a shower as his hair was sticking out in all directions, still slightly damp, and he was only wearing a pair of board shorts. Daisy's heart skipped a beat as she stopped on the top step and drank in the sight of him. Daisy dropped her bag and threw herself into his arms. They stood on the porch, arms entwined, bodies pushing up against each other as their lips sought each other, gentle at first, but growing more insistent as their kisses deepened. Dan's hand settled on the small of Daisy's back, scooping her in closer to him, while Daisy reached up with both hands to pull Dan's face closer to hers. Daisy could feel his heart beating in time with hers, as they gave in to the tension that had been building between them since they had kissed in the garden last week. After a few moments like this, Dan pulled back and looked down at Daisy with a grin.

"Would you like to come in?" he asked. Without

waiting for an answer, he reached down and picked up Daisy's bag, before scooping her up into his arms, kissing her again. Daisy laughed as he carried her inside, slamming the door closed.

Dan carried Daisy into his bedroom and carefully laid her on the bed.

"Hey Dan, there is something I have to tell you."

Dan was only half listening, and he pushed up her shirt and dropped his head to Daisy's belly.

"Dan, wait..." Daisy began, but it was too late. Dan had already seen the scars that ripped through the middle of Daisy's belly, tapering off around her left hip.

"Oh shit," Dan said, pulling away. "What the fuck happened to you?"

Daisy put her hands over her face, willing the tears to stop. This was her worst nightmare, and she couldn't believe she had let her guard down like this. Taking a deep breath, she opened her eyes and sat up.

"I tried to tell you the other day, I had a car crash a few years ago, and it left me with some really bad scars."

"Shit! That is messed up," said Dan. "Can I look?"

Reluctantly, Daisy lifted her shirt again and watched as Dan stared in fascination at her scar-puckered belly.

"Well, no wonder you always wear a rashie at the beach. I thought you were just being really sun smart." He leant forward to kiss Daisy's neck. "You know what...I mean, I still find you really sexy. We can turn the lights out and it shouldn't bother me."

Familiar tears of shame filled Daisy's eyes, and she pushed him away, upset that he didn't seem to understand that what he was saying was really hurtful.

"Dan, I'm really sorry. This is a big deal for me. I don't usually do this and the way you just spoke to me, it was kind of rude and I don't feel like sleeping with you right now."

"What? Seriously? Even though I said it doesn't bother me?"

"Hey Dan, sorry, but don't you see how insensitive you are being to me right now?" asked Daisy, confused by how Dan was acting and trying to explain how she felt.

Dan looked at Daisy, his usually calm face twisted up in a flash of anger. "I'm being insensitive? You come over and you get in my bed, acting like you were really into it, and then you change your mind." Dan stood up and grabbed a t-shirt from the hamper next to the bed. "Nah, fuck this."

Daisy watched Dan walk out of the room. *What the hell just happened*? She thought miserably. *How did this go so badly, so quickly?*

———

Daisy waited for a while to let Dan cool down before she joined him in the kitchen. She had made up her mind to go home to Royce and Arabella's if Dan was still acting strangely, and she wondered if Arabella had been right all along. Was there something weird about this guy?

But as she walked into the kitchen and saw Dan smiling down at his hungry dog, who was waiting patiently by her food bowl, she decided she had overreacted. This was Dan, after all, sweet Dan, who took her surfing every morning and built his grandmother a tropical garden.

Daisy smiled and bent down to scratch Costello behind the ears.

"Sorry for making you wait, Daisy, but I had a damsel in distress to rescue," Dan said, his voice back to normal now.

Daisy watched as Dan quickly fed Costello and poured them both some wine. He seemed to be back to his usual self, the earlier misunderstanding in the bedroom behind them. They chatted neutrally about the surf and Dan's work as they sat outside on the veranda, enjoying the balmy evening.

As the night deepened, Dan brought out a blanket, and they sat together on the outside lounge, the bottle of wine on the table in front of them and gentle music floating across the backyard from a neighboring party. A few small candles, burning merrily in the calm late summer night, lit up Dan's beautiful garden.

"I'm sorry about before Daisy. I just really like you and I get a bit overwhelmed by how I feel about you. I think I'm so excited that I get a few steps ahead of myself."

"That's ok. This is all new and we are still figuring out how we work together. I mean, Royce and Arabella have been together for years and they still don't always have it figured out."

As Daisy snuggled in closer to Dan's warm, strong body, she told him about Arabella and Royce's fight.

"They are usually so tight," she said, thinking back to their fight early that evening. "It scares me a bit because I always think of them as being the ones who have life totally under control, that it's just weirdos like me who don't know what they are doing. But if even they are not coping, how am I meant to cope?" Daisy looked up at Dan, her usually sparkly green eyes now sad.

"Change is hard! What if selling my business is like Arabella having a baby? What if it isn't what I think it will be? What if it's a mistake?"

"But change is also a huge part of life, Daisy," replied Dan, hugging her tighter. "If you hadn't decided to change, you might have not come to Bondi when you did, and then we would never have met."

"Now that would have been the biggest mistake of all," replied Daisy, reaching up to kiss him.

"I totally agree," Dan replied softly, before covering Daisy's lips with his own.

Seven

WhathappensinBondi...*The Bondi tribe was out in force this weekend! We spotted Bondi Babe Daisy Gardener getting chummy with wellness guru Fern Fasso, her live-in lover Louie T and some tasty friends on the veranda at Ravesis. Word on the street is that Fern is in talks with a certain international television production company to turn her life-style blog into a worldwide phenom. Yass Queen Fern—we are here for your global domination!*

Finally, it was the Sydney Fashion Festival. Daisy was still undecided about what to do with her business. Between the three of them, Daisy, AB and Royce had come up with enough money to make a dent in the Gardiner's next repayment. It was nowhere near enough, but it meant that Daisy could still keep her options open for now. Mostly Daisy was looking forward to seeing the glamorous creations on show during the festival and she was relieved that this self-imposed deadline for making up her mind had finally arrived.

Hopefully, after this week, I'll know what the hell I am doing with my life, she mused, as she stood looking at her wardrobe, assessing the glamorous dress she was about to wear to the glamorous party. She had decided to wait until the end of the week after all to decide, and instead had thrown herself into preparing for this opening night extravaganza.

As was tradition, the launch of the Sydney Fashion Festival was being held at Carriageworks, the industrial train sheds turned art and function space just to the south of the city. The opening night of Fashion Festival was a spectacle, topped only by the White Party, the event's swimwear showcase and closing party, held at Bondi's Icebergs Pool.

The theme for the opening night party was simply 'Night' and guests were encouraged to match their outfit to the concept, as elegantly and imaginatively as possible. As a designer and dress maker in her own right, Daisy had jumped at the chance to create an outfit for the evening. Luckily, Dan's grandmother had owned a beautiful old sewing machine, which was still functioning perfectly, thanks to years of loving maintenance by Dan's grandparents, and he was more than happy to let her use it to sew her gown. Dan and Costello had sat and watched Daisy as she measured and cut and tweaked and sewed, interrupting her now and then to bring her cups of tea and distract her with kisses.

This year, Arabella and Daisy were going to both parties as guests. Royce was working at the opening party, having been commissioned to document the behind-the-scenes preparation and buzz of bringing together Australia's top designers and models all in place.

Arabella had confided in Daisy that she was really looking forward to going out and not working for a change. Tension between her and Royce remained, despite their first honest conversation about the baby, and they were still acting a little frosty towards each other. Arabella admitted that things had been pretty tough for her lately. Daisy had asked if having her stay was putting more pressure on them, to which Arabella had hurriedly replied not at all.

Now the big night was finally here. Daisy and Arabella emerged from their Uber and headed down the red carpet. Daisy's dress was made from inky midnight blue silk, with a strapless bodice and a full three-quarter skirt. Tiny hand sewn crystals had been sewn across the dress, creating the illusion of stars winking in and out of view. She had also made a matching headpiece, adorned with star-shaped crystals, worn somewhere between a crown and a headband. The pale gems sparkled against her dark hair. A pair of Arabella's strappy midnight blue heels complemented the look.

Beside her, Arabella was wearing a black silk jumpsuit, on loan from Alice McCall, which plunged to her naval, where a Swarovski crystal encrusted silver moon hid the roundness of her just showing baby bump. She too was wearing strappy heels—silver and encrusted with crystals - and a star-shaped clutch. Both Daisy and Arabella were very pleased with their efforts, and they strutted confidently down the red carpet and into the party.

Inside, they mingled with movie and tv stars,

designers and socialites and Daisy still couldn't get over how many celebrities seemed to live at the parties Arabella took her to. Lozza Rothermere-Smythe was there, along with most of the Lost at Sea guests and what seemed like every major Australian Hollywood star. Daisy's eyes popped when she spotted Hugh Jackman on the other side of the room, and she'd choked up in awe when Collette Dinigan stopped by to say hello to Arabella. For a moment she thought she'd had her photo taken with Isla Fischer and Rebel Wilson until she realised the photographer was strategically positioning her behind an ivy-covered pillar. But it didn't really matter—Daisy had arrived at her first major fashion show, and it was love at first click of the camera.

The best moment of the night however, and possibly Daisy's whole life, came when an ethereal blonde woman had tapped her on the shoulder to complement her dress and ask who the designer was.

"It's actually a piece I created for the party tonight," Daisy had replied, shyly at first but becoming more animated the more she spoke about her designs. "It was such a fun concept, and I had this great piece of fabric from this organic Cambodian silk farm that I was dying to use... it's run by these young Buddhist nuns, and they use their profits to train young women to become silk farmers and weavers, it's such a great organisation...so it all just fell into place for tonight!"

"Oh, I love that you've combined such an elegant design with such a socially aware supplier. The fashion world needs more ethically sourced labels like yours. Look, here's my email address, please put me on your mailing list and let me know when you are ready to show your first collection."

"Oh my gosh, that was Cate Blanchett!" asked Daisy breathlessly, once the blonde woman had glided serenely away. "Oh my gosh, Cate Blanchett likes my dress!"

"Of course she did," Arabella said, smiling proudly at Daisy. "You're a talented designer! Come on, we need to say hello to Roxy, and I am sure I saw Zoe Foster-Blake before..."

As Daisy followed Arabella through the crowd, she saw Royce briefly, when he followed a lighting technician out on to the stage to test a spotlight. He was shooting intensely but waved to them when he saw them walking into the seating area. Daisy watched her brother work, filled with the same sense of pride she'd had when she visited him on the shoot a few weeks earlier. She loved seeing how successful he had become, and she was so happy that he had found a job that he loved.

Soon it was time for them to take their seats, second row from the front, and the lights dimmed. Magnolia bushes lit up with fairy lights dotted the stage, and jasmine vines were languidly draped across the backdrop, creating a riot of sweet fragrance throughout the room. Peacocks and nightingales chirped and strutted on the backdrop of ferns and vines cascading from the ceiling on either side of the stage. Across the ceiling above them, constellation after constellation of sparkling stars popped out, one by one, until the entire room felt wild and untamed, like a personal dream garden.

The music began, a gentle, opulent remix of children's lullabies, woven with the thrilling birdsong of the peacocks and nightingales. Nan Sinclair, dressed in an avian inspired turquoise dress, strode out on to the stage. Daisy gasped. The dress glistened as Nan strode elegantly along the runway, its long and sleek body tapering out into a train of feathers. The outfit was completed by a sparkling, feathered collar rising high above her head, and a delicate gold crown perched jauntily on her smooth, dark hair. It was exquisite and, although completely impractical as actual clothing; it was a work of art. Daisy sat enthralled as creation after creation was shimmied down the runway.

Arabella watched her best friend fondly as she took in the outfits dreamed up by some of the most creative fashion designers in Australia, more art than fashion, and all riffing on the same theme of Night.

"I knew you'd love this," she said, leaning closer to Daisy so she could be heard over the music. "It's so good to be sitting down for a change and letting everyone else do the work!"

After the runway show was over, the party began in earnest. Daisy and Arabella wandered through the famous crowd, eating the canapés and drinking the delicious champagne. Royce was still working backstage, photographing the aftermath and the pack down of the racks of fashion masterpieces. Daisy was keeping Dan updated throughout the night via text and the odd sneaky photo.

Check it out! It's Kylie!

Is she spinning around?

I think she is... wait, no, she's just locomoting out of here...

You are lame-o Gardiner, LAME-O!

Ha! You wish you were me!

No, I wish you were here... guess what I'd do?

Daisy read Dan's text message with a smile, before blushing and stifling a giggle at his following, much more graphic text.

Stop it! Gotta go make out with Hugh Jackman! she replied, before putting her phone away, not waiting for a reply.

An hour later, Daisy found herself standing in a group of famous designers, chatting with Jack Finnigan, the team from surf label Glass, and the Amerlaine sisters, her personal idols given how similar their early trajectory had been. Arabella was chatting animatedly with Mike Sokolov and his breakfast show host, Katrina Kellogg. It was the most surreal moment of Daisy's life, and she was mentally taking notes as she listened to the designers reminisce about their early days in the fashion business.

"I cut all the patterns for my first show in my mum's garage," laughed Jack. "We had no space in the actual studio to lay out the designs, so we had to carry everything out to Marrickville from Paddo and back again on the bus!"

"Gigi, remember being so broke that first season that we were unpicking the dresses off our back to scrape together enough fabric to put together the toiles?"

"My first job was literally sweeping the floor and getting coffee at Darla Impala's salon!"

"But wasn't it worth it when you got that first show or your first sale?" asked Daisy, hanging on to every word the designers were saying.

Jack Finnigan leaned towards Daisy with a warm smile and squeezed her arm. "Nothing in my life will beat the first time I watched my designs walk the runway! And it doesn't go away, you know, that feeling of 'oh my goodness, how did I get here?' But that moment, when you are right on the edge of something huge, hold on to that feeling for as long as you can. Because that's the best feeling in the world!"

Standing in the middle of the heaving, glittery room, Daisy felt inspired and excited. She felt like she was really on the right track. Everything these world-famous designers were saying to her made her feel like she was in the right place.

Daisy wasn't sure what it was about these creative types that intrigued her the most. *Was it their impressive catalogue of creations? Or was it more that, like Royce, they had found something they were really good at, something they loved and they had created a world out of it?* Daisy loved creating, sewing, and making. She loved the feel of fabric in her hands, loved feeling how different the texture of silk was to fresh cotton, and how the fabric pulled and ripped in different directions. She loved assembling fabric in different ways, making it work differently than expected, and she wondered if this meant she was one of them, a designer.

These people are speaking my language, she realised suddenly and smiled quietly to herself as she imagined the possibilities of what that meant.

Not long after the directors from Glass had excused themselves and Arabella had disappeared to use the bathroom for the tenth time that night, a commotion on the other side of the room made Daisy look up. Suddenly, all the hairs on her arms began to prickle and a collective gasp echoed across the room. It could only mean one thing... Mack Boddington had arrived.

Daisy watched in awe as Mack made his way through the crowd, over to where she was standing. As he sauntered across the room, the crowd parted, giving the impression he was gliding on air, rather than walking across the repurposed concrete slabs of Carriagework's main hall.

As he drew alongside their group, he smiled broadly in their direction, before air kissing each of the assembled fashion celebs. Daisy's eyes grew in size as she again stood next to Australia's most handsome television star. Of course, she was crazy about Dan, but how often was she going to get bask in the radiated glory of the next Brad Pitt?

Daisy was so entranced that she didn't catch Mack's first words, nor see the horrified expressions of those closest to her.

"Martini love, thanks," he said, clicking his fingers before turning his back to her.

"I'm sorry?" asked Daisy, blinking in confusion. "What?"

"I'm sorry, what?" he imitated, with a sarcastic laugh. He looked at her for a moment before continuing. "Oh, right, you didn't hear me. I'll have a martini, thanks."

"You want me to get you a drink?" Daisy replied, looking around at the assembled group, still confused but with the growing feeling that someone was playing a horrible prank on her. She looked around for Arabella, but she was nowhere to be seen.

"I asked you to get me a martini. You are a waitress, no? Your job is to wait on the guests of party. Procuring drinks is not hard. Since it's your job and your job is to get me drinks. And can you send over a better-looking waitress please? Thanks!"

He flicked his hand as if to say off you go. But Daisy

didn't move, she was too shocked by the rude encounter to move.

There was an awkward silence as Mack glanced at Daisy and then around at the group.

"Why aren't you moving? Bloody hell, the service here is terrible!"

Finally someone, Daisy wasn't sure who, explained that she was a guest at the party.

Daisy awkwardly stuck her hand out. "Actually, we met a few weeks ago, I'm Arabella McCarthy's sister-in-law."

Mack ignored her hand and instead looked her up and down. "You're a guest?" he asked incredulously. "But who invited you?" Mack turned away to look at the other celebrities, who were all shaking their heads and telling him to not be such an idiot.

But Mack wasn't listening. Just as Arabella returned to the group and the music lulled, Mack turned back to Daisy and announced loudly. "Listen, sorry, you just don't look like the type of person who would be invited here as a guest, you know, you're not famous, you're too big and to be honest, not really hot enough..." Mack trailed off and threw his arms around Arabella. "Arabella darling, thank goodness you are here, a true beauty, now the party can really start!"

A ripple of gasps went through the crowd but the music picked up again and it was soon forgotten as more drinks were served. The gathered celebrities drifted away into the crowd and Mack grabbed Arabella's arm and towed her away towards the bar, leaving Daisy alone with an empty plate.

She stood still for a moment, blinking back the hot tears that were threatening to spill down her cheeks. She didn't really believe Mack's cruel comments, she was far too self-confident to let that worry her. What she was really upset about was that he had embarrassed her in front of so many interesting and cool people, people that she hoped to work with one day. They had fled the scene of the crime, not wanting to be left alone with the awkwardness. Daisy also noted grimly that none of them had really stood up for her or checked that she was ok. Daisy felt humiliated.

I have to get out of here, she thought desperately, casting her eyes around for a quick escape.

Daisy spotted a fire door and saw her exit stage left. She grabbed a bottle of the very expensive champagne in defiance and slipped out the door, not seeing that it was alarmed and connected to the overhead sprinkler system. Not that she would have cared if she had noticed.

Daisy kept her tears of humiliation from spilling until she burst out into the gloomy, rainy night, unaware of the chaos unfolding on the opening night of Sydney Fashion Festival,

Dammit, she cursed, looking up at the sky as hot tears finally coursed down over her cheeks. Her phone beeped frantically. It was Arabella.

Babe, where are you? Are you ok? Water is everywhere and Mack is losing it- give me 10 and I'll come find you.

I'm going home, texted Daisy in reply, oblivious to the throng of panicked celebrities exiting the party on the other side of the building. *I'm ok, really, go take care of Mack and enjoy the rest of the night.*

Taking shelter from the pouring rain at a bus stop, Daisy ordered an Uber and pulled herself together.

What a dick, she thought tiredly. Her feet hurt from

the beautiful but impractical shoes and her head was pounding from all the champagne.

The Uber driver handed her a bottle of water as she wearily climbed into the car.

"Hi Daisy, is it? I'm Dave. Looks like it was quite a night," he observed kindly, as he set off toward the beach.

"I'm glad I don't have to do that all the time!" Daisy replied. "To be quite honest, I just wish I was at home watching Netflix in my pyjamas!"

"Your wish is my command madam, I'll have you there as soon as possible!" replied Dave cheerily and Daisy settled back into the comfortable seat of the car, watching as the streetlights shimmered and slipped by, as the slick, inky black streets of Redfern turned into Surry Hills and then Paddington.

For the first time since coming down to stay with Royce and Arabella, Daisy felt a pang of homesickness for her kind and simple life back up the coast. She thought back to that night on the balcony, when Arabella had won the Mack Boddington contract. She remembered feeling so happy and delighted with the world that night. The breeze had been warm and the four of them had laughed so much. Daisy realised that was what she really wanted. To be happy and laughing somewhere warm, with the people who loved her the most.

"I have to sell my business," she blurted, surprising herself by how good it felt to say the words out loud. It felt right, she realised with a start, because it was right. "I have no idea what I will do instead, but I know I never want to have another night like this, ever again."

"Awesome!" Dave replied, smiling at Daisy through the

rear-view mirror. "Sometimes it doesn't matter that you don't know where you are going, just as long as you know you are going somewhere."

"That is so true, Dave," replied Daisy. "That is so true!"

Feeling more settled than she had in ages, Daisy relaxed as the car whisked her down Old South Head Road, and back to the salty air of Bondi Beach.

EIGHT

———

Daisy woke the next morning with a clear heart. She lay in bed for a minute, relishing the softness of the bed as she thought about her decision to sell the business.

"I don't want that life," she said out loud. "I want Dan and I want Costello and Elvis and the beach."

Although she would have been happy to stay cocooned in her bed forever, a short growl of hunger told her it was time to get up and find some breakfast. She also had to find Arabella to tell her the news. She was slowly becoming aware of voices coming from the lounge and the annoying hum of several lawnmowers in the distance. *Who mows at 7am on a Sunday?*

Daisy got out of bed and threw on a dressing gown and wandered wearily out into the kitchen.

As her eyes adjusted to the gloom, Daisy stopped dead in her tracks, momentarily breathless as she took in the sight before her.

Mack Boddington, the man she hoped never to see again, was standing in the middle of Royce and Arabella's living room, his stormy eyes, dark and unreadable, fixed solely on her.

Hackles raised and heart pounding, Daisy wasn't sure if she wanted to kiss him or punch him. Arabella and her assistant, Lucy, were pacing around the living room. Royce was sitting at the table calmly reading the paper and drinking a cup of coffee, trying not to laugh at the ridiculous tableau playing out before him.

"What the hell is he doing here?" Daisy asked finally. As last night's humiliation came rushing back at the sight of Mack, she decided she would very much like to punch his smug, handsome face.

"Hey babe, sorry, I hope we didn't wake you. We've had some trouble," said Arabella, rubbing her belly and gesturing towards Mack. "After Mack's foot in mouth disease kicked in and you left, we got evacuated out of Carriageworks when the fire alarm sprinklers went off."

Arabella paused and glanced speculatively at her best

friend. "You didn't have anything to do with that did you?" she asked with a tight smile.

Daisy vaguely remembered seeing a warning sign on the fire door she'd escaped through last night. It was probably her fault. But instead of confessing, she shook her head and didn't say anything.

"So we were all outside in the rain, waiting to be given the all clear by the police and the fire brigade, when dummy here got busted by the police snorting cocaine off the...off the unmentionables.... of a young man, in a portaloo, at a construction site across the road," Arabella continued.

"Stop saying it like that, you know he was 23! Plus, everyone was doing it!"

Arabella stopped and glared at Mack. "Shut up Mack. Just shut up. Not everyone was doing it. And not everyone is waiting for the ink to dry on not one, but two Hollywood contracts! How could you be so bloody stupid!"

Daisy took a cup of coffee from Royce, who winked conspiratorially at her, and walked to the window to see what all the noise was. *That is so loud for lawnmowers.*

As she drew the curtains across, she was shocked to see a crowd of paparazzi standing across the small street, jostling for the best view into their apartment. Overhead, several helicopters and one persistent drone hovered as close as possible to the balcony, while down on the water several speed boats were bobbing up and down, with large camera lenses trained directly on where Daisy stood in the door frame. She shut the curtains quickly and turned around.

"Oh my goodness Mack, you are in trouble," she said sarcastically.

"Who are you?" Mack asked impatiently.

Daisy rolled her eyes. "You don't remember? Last night at the Fashion Festival party? I'm the waitress who was too fat to serve you drinks."

Royce looked up from his paper, "Wait, what? What happened?" He looked at his sister and his wife in confusion.

Meanwhile, Mack was looking Daisy up and down, a calculating look taking over his face.

"Oh right, you're that little hippy girl, aren't you," he said vaguely, a sneaky look taking over his face. "The one that has been in all the papers. What's your name? Gardenia?"

Before anyone could protest, he came up behind Daisy and turned her around, encircling her waist with his arms and nuzzling into her neck.

"I have an idea," he said wickedly, ripping open the curtains and waving to the waiting media scrum.

Daisy stood still for a moment, shocked by how good the warmth of Mack's breath on her neck felt, as the barrage of camera flashes and screams from the assembled crowd outside the flat and the helicopters and drones hovering at eye level increased to fever pitch. But she quickly recovered her composure when she remembered whose arms were around her. Even just the touch of him was making her feel sick, and she turned and fled back into the relative safety of the dark kitchen.

"What the hell!" exclaimed Royce, jumping to his feet.

"Arabella, can we somehow leak it to the press that I snuck out of the party last night, with this little flower girl here and they fingered the wrong guy last night? That I've fallen for this wholesome child and was home laying my hands on her perfectly legal, perfectly appropriate little body the whole time?"

"Don't say fingered," retorted Arabella, "Not after last night."

"Oh Mack," gasped Lucy. "That's genius! You are a genius!"

"No way, Mack, you can't bring Daisy into this. This is your mess, and you have to figure it out. Daisy is not here to fix things for you!" said Royce hotly.

He walked over to the door, putting his arm up to ward over the onslaught of flashes still going off outside, and tried to pull the curtain across. But Mack was enjoying showing off to his adoring public too much, and so the curtain remained partially opened.

"Shut up, everyone!" Daisy all but shouted. She looked over at Mack, who was now standing in the balcony doorway, showing of his impeccable washboard abs to the assembled media. "What makes you think I would do anything to help you? You are seriously the biggest dickhead I have ever met, Mack. There is no way in the world I would help you out."

Daisy turned to her best friend and rolled her eyes. "Can you believe this guy? As if I would. Anyway, I decided after last night's drama that this life is just not for me. I'm not cut out for it. I am going to sell and go home, where I belong, and figure out what I am going to do next."

Arabella looked out at the photographers and back at the young actor standing in the balcony doorway. "Daisy," she said slowly, "I know you are ready to sell, but if you do this for us, just for a few weeks until the scandal dies down, your company will be worth triple what it is now, and you would have more than enough for Lola and Bill and for you. You could walk away never having to work on anything you didn't want to, ever again. But you don't have to. Babe, if you don't want to, I will never ask you about it again, but just think about it for a minute, ok?"

"Wait, do you need some money? I have money..." interrupted Mack.

"Stay out of this Mack, you are not helping," warned Arabella.

"No, seriously, I have lots of money. How much do you need? 50k? 100?"

Daisy looked up at Mack, startled at how casually he was throwing around large amounts of money.

"What? Of course not, we are not degenerates like you. I just need $18,000 for my parents. For their mortgage."

Mack looked down at Daisy quickly, an odd look flashing across his face.

"You can have it."

Daisy looked up at Mack in confusion. "What do you mean?

"I mean it, the money is yours."

"Wait, are you offering to pay Daisy $18,000 dollars to be your fake girlfriend?" asked Royce in disbelief.

Mack looked from Royce to Daisy. "If that is what you need. Be my fake girlfriend and I will give you $18,000 dollars."

Mack was looking at Daisy with an intensity she'd never seen before. She stared out at the scrum, mulling over the idea of being financially secure for once. Paying off her parent's debt. Maybe going to university finally.

She had to admit, the idea of a large pay out was enticing. And having Mack's money to pay the bank straight away was icing on the cake. *Wait, am I insane for even considering this?*

"What would it mean? What would I have to do?" she asked Arabella, eventually.

"You and Mack would go on a series of 'dates' over the next few weeks. Take him paddle boarding, eat some fairy floss at Luna Park. There's the Bay to Beach fun run coming up next week—you guys could compete in that. Lots of wholesome, healthy dates, where you get to show off your sexy bods in the sunshine."

Daisy thought about it some more. "He pays for everything right." That was a demand, not a question.

"Absolutely."

Daisy looked at Mack. "We don't actually have to touch each other, do we?"

Arabella looked across at their body language. Mack was sulking at the dining table now and Daisy was standing on the opposite side of the room, arms crossed defensively.

"Well...you will have to make it look believable, you know, when you are in love with someone you want to touch them," Arabella avoided Royce's pointed gaze.

"And we spin it so that it looks like we decided long distance wasn't going to work out. Once the deals are signed and I can fade back into obscurity?"

"Absolutely," Arabella said again, feeling more confident with every one of Daisy's questions.

Finally, Daisy asked her last question, the one she'd been dreading.

"What about Dan?"

"You would have to take a break from him…just for a few weeks. Then you guys can pick up where you were…"

Daisy winced at the suggestion, her heart contracting at the thought of not being able to see Dan for a few weeks.

"Daisy, you don't have to do this!" said Royce angrily, before turning to his wife. "AB, this is out of control. You can't ask Daisy to do this!"

"This is going to benefit her just as much as it is going to benefit Mack," replied Arabella hotly. "And this is also my business I am protecting! This is my last shot at doing something big!"

"Oh, this is such a marvellous idea," cooed Lucy, oblivious to the tension between Arabella and Royce, and Daisy's discomfort.

Mack was getting excited again, and he had come over to where Daisy was standing, trying to wrap his arms around her. "Yes, come on Gardenia, this is a marvellous idea! Say yes! Take my money and take me as your new faux beau!"

"Stop it! Everyone, just shut up while I think!" shouted Daisy, pushing Mack's arms away.

After a minute, she turned to face Arabella, Royce, Mack and Lucy.

"Ok. I'll do it. But I have three conditions. One, that Dan is ok with it. I am going to go over and see him now, and I will let you know this afternoon."

"Great," enthused Arabella, "If he is ok, we will start with a sunset fish and chips dinner at the beach, just the two of you and some nice cushions and lanterns. Lucy, can you call some discreet friends who could loan us some products in exchange for some media placement?"

"AB!" protested Royce. "She hasn't said yes yet!"

"What is your second condition, my beautiful queen Gardeeen?"

"Second, Mack, you have to pay me the money today. In fact, I want you to transfer it into my account right now."

Daisy turned to face Mack properly, her breath catching as he stared back at her, his blue eyes dark and ominous. "I mean it, Mack, right now."

"Right now? What if your boyfriend won't let you? How do I know I will get my money back?" he asked quietly.

Daisy glared up at Mack. "Do you want my help or not?"

"Fine, fine, I'll do now," Mack replied, unlocking his mobile phone and opening his online bank app. "Put your account details in then."

Daisy quickly typed in her BSB and account number and shoved the phone back at Mack, who was suddenly smiling again.

"Well, now that that is settled, what is your third condition, my beautiful queen Gardeeen?"

"That you stop using made up nicknames and use my actual name."

"Which is?" Mack looked around the room, confused.

"My name is Daisy, you fucking jerk!" she shouted angrily, throwing the last of her cold coffee into Mack's smug, handsome face. "My name is Daisy!"

———

A few moments later, Daisy sat on her bed, wondering what the hell she had just done. *Was this the dumbest thing she had ever agreed to?* She took a few deep breaths to calm down, before turning her mind to how she was going to tell Dan the news.

A soft tap at the door interrupted her reverie. Her brother poked his head around the door. "Oh Royce, thank goodness it's you! Come in and close the door!" she said, gesturing to the bed next to her.

Royce sat down and looked worriedly at his sister. "Are you really sure you are ok with this?" he asked, reaching out to squeeze Daisy's hand.

"Nope!" she replied honestly, her eyes brimming with tears. "I don't really know at all. I know this is a great opportunity for AB. And we can help Mum and Dad today. And I know this could be so good for my shop and for us as a family, if I can make a good sale out of it. But it feels weird. And I know Dan is going to be so hurt by all of this..." Daisy trailed off, lost in thought for a moment.

"Daisy, listen. I know I said a lot of things out there. But I just want you to know that no matter what you choose and no matter whether that decision turns out to be the best or the worst thing for you to do, I'll always be here for you. And although it is great and amazing that you are considering Mum and Dad, and AB's career and Dan's feelings right now, you have to do what is right for you."

Royce reached out to hug his sister tight.

"I love you, kiddo. You are the best middle sister a guy could ask for. Please just promise me you will make this decision based on what you want. Based on what you want to do."

As Royce left the room, Daisy closed her eyes for a moment, thinking about Royce's advice. Perhaps it was time to make a choice. As soon as she thought it, she smiled, feeling like a weight had been lifted.

Ok then. Let's get this over with.

———

After texting Dan that she was on her way over, Daisy had a quick shower, jumped on Arabella's bike, and rode down to Forest Knoll Avenue. Buoyed by her talk with Royce, she felt like she had made the right decision and she was glad to have something to do.

But when Dan met her at the front door, he kissed her hungrily, and for a second she felt her resolve waver as she melted into his arms.

What if I just ignore Mack, ignore AB and the money, and just stay here, kissing this beautiful guy forever, she thought wistfully, before pulling away and leading him out onto the back deck. A fresh pot of coffee waited for them, but Daisy wished it was something a little stronger, like a pot of tequila or whiskey. *Anything to give me the courage to say what I am about to say.*

Daisy was sure that anything this difficult to say was probably a bad thing to do. But there was so much tied up in this. It wasn't just about the money, although that would make things easier. There was also Arabella to consider, and Daisy didn't want to hurt her best friend.

No, she had to try to explain this to Dan.

"What happened to you last night?" Dan asked, once they were seated, coffee in hand.

"It turned out to be a pretty shitty evening," said Daisy.

"Really? But it seemed like you were having a great time? Don't tell me Hugh turned out to be a total bore and followed you around all night?"

Daisy smiled at his lame joke and shook her head.

"The party was evacuated because I accidentally opened a fire escape and set off the sprinklers. That was after Mack Boddington insulted me and called me an ugly, fat waitress in front of all the really cool designers. So, then I went home, but Arabella stayed with Mack and he got busted snorting cocaine off a young guy's, you know, extremities."

Daisy gestured down at Dan's lap with a hint of a grin, before sighing.

"Oh man, it was a ridiculous night. It sounds so stupid now that I am saying it out loud," she continued, postponing the inevitable.

"That sounds awful! Bloody hell, Daisy, those people are so full of themselves. I don't know how cool people like Royce and AB live in that world. What terrible things to say to someone! I reckon you're pretty alright and you'll do me just fine." Dan took her hand and smiled, his eyes crinkling in the way that made Daisy's belly flip flop every time she saw it.

"Daisy, I..."

"No! Stop! Don't say that yet! I haven't finished..." said Daisy in a panic.

"But you went home? What else happened?" he diverted gently.

Daisy took a deep breath.

"So, this morning, I woke up, and AB and Royce and Mack and AB's assistant were all at the flat. And they needed some scheme to make Mack look wholesome again and so I said I would pretend to be his girlfriend…"

"What?" Dan pulled away, confused.

Tears filled Daisy's eyes now, spilling down her cheeks. "It's just to help make the shop more profitable. But only if you are ok with it!"

Dan stood up and moved over to the veranda railing where he stood, raking his fingers through his hair.

"I don't understand. You are going to pretend to be Mack's girlfriend because he is a dickhead and got in trouble and in exchange for that, it will make your shop worth more money?"

Daisy nodded at Dan's recounting of the mess, wincing at how vacuous and selfish it all sounded.

"It's also for AB and my parents…I really need to help her out because she is so scared this baby is going to mean the end of her career and if I do, then I will have enough money to help my parents and save their house…"

"Is money really that important to you?" Dan interrupted. "Because I didn't think you were the kind of person who cared about stuff like that."

Daisy stopped picking at her fingernail and looked up at Dan, whose expression had changed. He was glaring at her now, his usually kind eyes flashing with anger and jealousy.

"That's not fair Dan. You know my parents are not well off and they sacrificed so much for me. All my life, all I've ever been is a market stall holder and a shop manager. This is it. This is my chance to never have to struggle again and to make it up to my family. I don't care about the fame, I care about the financial security. We don't all inherit houses in Bondi, you know!" Daisy stopped and took a breath. "Sorry, that was unfair," she said glumly.

Dan stood in the sunshine on the veranda, thinking over Daisy's words.

"I don't like this Daisy. I thought you were my girl. I don't want to see another guy with his hands all over you. That's not how this should work."

"Dan, I know this is hard, but I'm not anyone's 'girl' and it isn't like that at all. Besides, it wouldn't be real. Trust me, Mack is a jerk and the less he has his hands on me the better!"

"Come off it Daisy. You've always had a thing for him. Just admit it. Have you already slept with him? I mean, you're not sleeping with me, so you must be sleeping with someone."

Daisy stood up, angry again. "What the hell! Dan, I am so sorry this is so hard for you. But I came here to talk to you about it and make a decision together. I didn't think you'd be so rude about it. I didn't think you'd insult me."

Dan was silent for a moment and Daisy gathered her things, ready to leave.

"Wait," Dan said finally. "I'm sorry, that was uncalled for."

Daisy sat still, staring out at the garden, not daring to look him in the eye.

"So it's only for two weeks?" he continued, looking at Daisy doubtfully.

"Yep,"

"And it's totally fake? You really don't secretly love him?"

Daisy shook her head, thinking to herself sadly that love was the last thing on her mind right now.

Dan stepped forward and pulled Daisy to her feet. "Before I say yes, I am going to kiss you, in the vain hope that kissing me might change your mind."

"Dan, I really should go," she replied, looking up at him with sad, green eyes, still confused about the way he had reacted to her news.

But Dan leant forward and covered Daisy's lips softly, his own barely moving against her skin. Gently, and more insistently, he kissed her. It wasn't urgent, it was slow and tender and made Daisy's heart ache in a way she had never felt before. But she didn't kiss him back.

After what seemed like a lifetime, Dan pulled away and cupped Daisy's face in his hands.

"Listen to me, if that jerk is bad to you, I will punch his lights out!"

"If that jerk is bad to me, there won't be much left of him to punch," she replied with a shaky laugh. She looked up at Dan's deadly serious face. "But I'll save some for you anyway, just for fun."

Later, as Daisy walked down the steps to her bike, Dan suddenly called out after her.

"Daisy, wait."

Daisy stopped and turned around. Dan was still standing on the porch, leaning up against the edge of the railing, his arms crossed tightly.

"I'm really sorry for before," he said, despondently. "Please don't forget about me."

"I won't. It's only for two weeks. But Dan, I don't think we should see each other until this is over. I think it's just going to hurt you and make me feel really awful. Is that ok?"

Dan nodded in agreement and sat down on the front porch, hugging Costello tightly.

"I've got a bad feeling about this doggo," he said sadly, as he and Costello watched the girl they loved ride away down the street, into the arms of another man. "I've got a bad, bad feeling about this."

Nine

WhathappensinBondi...*Was that Bondi babe Daisy Gardiner and bad boy Mack Boddington we saw getting cosy on the beach at sunset yesterday? Sources tell us things are hotting up for this surprising and sexy new couple!*

———

A few days later, Arabella and Daisy were sitting at the dining room table, going over the schedule of activities that Mack and Arabella had put together. Since Daisy had tearfully arrived back from Dan's house, Arabella and Lucy had been relentless in their organisation of Daisy's fake love affair, trying to keep Daisy busy and keep her mind off her temporary break from Dan.

It had all started with the fish and chips picnic on the beach that first night, Mack and Daisy's first official 'date'. It felt more like a photoshoot, with designer rugs and cushions, soft lamplights, and ornate plastic wine glasses. Even the evening weather followed Arabella's strict instructions, showing off with a pink and teal sunset and an accompanying soft warm breeze. Unfortunately for Daisy, it turned out to be a real photoshoot, as Arabella had tipped off several paparazzi and had erected a small photography platform behind them and to the left, positioned so that they could catch the couple canoodling against the romantic sunset glowing across the sky. As they walked down to the sand, carrying a bag full of blankets and wine, Mack took hold of Daisy's hand and gave her some uncharacteristically kind advice about how to deal with the paparazzi.

"Just smile a lot, but don't smile with a wide smile. That always ends up looking weird. If it gets too hard, just lean in close. I'll wrap my arms around you, and you'll be a bit more protected from the cameras."

"Thanks," she replied cautiously, her hand tingling as Mack stroked his thumb against her palm. He coughed a few times as they walked, glancing around uncomfortably.

"Umm, listen, Daisy, about last night. I was really drunk at the party. I really didn't mean those things I said to you. They are clearly not true. I was just drunk and stupid, I guess."

Daisy stiffened and tried to pull her hand away, but Mack kept a tight grip. "Careful, the cameras are already here."

He looked down at her. He was smiling, but his eyes looked tired and just a little sad. "I'm not stupid, you know."

"What do you mean?" Daisy asked, unsure what he was trying to say.

"I heard what you said about me at the Lost at Sea party. I'm not stupid. I actually have a master's degree in

American Literature. I was hurt and mad at you. But that's no excuse to treat you the way I did last night. I am really sorry. I was way out of line. I'd like to say that I'm not really like that but seems that's not true these days. So, I'm sorry."

Daisy flushed and looked up at the man beside her in surprise. So he had heard her, after all. She started to feel bad but then remembered that he was an actor. Could a throwaway comment from a no one like her really have upset him that much?

"I'm sorry too," she replied carefully. "I didn't really think that anything I could say could actually hurt someone like you. You always seem pretty tough and sure of yourself."

"Things are never what they seem in this bubble of celebrity," he replied contemplatively. "But it's ok, I get it. I am a jerk usually. But shall we call a truce for now?"

Daisy nodded and smiled tentatively before pulling back, confused. "Wait, you have a master's degree in American Literature?"

Mack nodded.

"But that is so impressive. Seriously, why don't you talk about it more?"

Mack shrugged. "It's my thing, not anyone else's."

By now, they had reached their date, and they each took a seat on the lavish picnic rug. Mack poured her a glass of wine and started chatting inanely about how exciting the launch of the Fashion Festival had been. The cameras lapped it up.

Daisy had never felt more uncomfortable, but she smiled through it, hiding her face in the crook of Mack's navy cable knit jumper when it got too much. Luckily this only made it look as though she was shyly snuggling into her new lover's arm and the press lapped it up.

Mack and Daisy, it's true love! Screamed the headlines.

Mack Boddington, Australian television heartthrob confirms love affair with Byron Bay fashion mogul!

Boho babe Daisy Gardiner snags her own Aussie superstar!

Buoyed by the success of Daisy and Mack's first public outing, Arabella had set a gruelling schedule of days filled with sporty, wholesome goodness and nights overflowing with all the glitz and glam that Sydney had to offer.

Every morning, Mack would arrive at the flat, his arms full of luscious looking fruit. They would then swap it out for some green juices Arabella had picked up earlier and walk down to Icebergs for morning yoga, before hitting the coastal track for a quick jog to Tama and back. Daisy pointed out that she was quite ok at making her own smoothies, especially with all the fruit piling up from Mack's staged early morning arrivals (Ok, she admitted, he did look pretty hot on the intercom, wearing nothing but a pair of boardies and a box full of pineapples and mangos) but Arabella wanted the colours of the juices to be just right.

When asked about his newfound love of the outdoors and if he had renounced his partying ways, Mack recited the story Arabella had concocted for them, about how when they had met Mack hadn't believed that Daisy could run ten kilometres faster than he could and she had challenged him to run the Bay to Beach fun-run with her and raise some much needed funds for the Children's Medical Research Institute at Westmead Hospital.

"Turns out she is a speed demon and I've needed to go into some serious training just to keep up," he'd joked as they were accosted by photographers on their way to Tamarama.

After their wholesome mornings, they would then have a much-needed afternoon to themselves - by then Daisy would be ready to throttle Mack - before getting ready to go out to a series of cool parties, dripping with actors and models and DJs. Daisy would wear something she had made, and Mack would spin her around the red carpet, pointing out how gorgeous she looked and giving her the chance to show off her design skills to an ever-increasing audience.

After a week of this, it seemed that the world had forgiven and forgotten Mack's Fashion Festival launch party transgressions. The celebrity blogs and daily newspapers were in love with 'Maisy' as they had become affectionately known, and Daisy was now being asked for just as many autographs as Mack. They seemed to be everywhere. From paddle-boarding at Rose Bay, to having dinner at Lentil as Anything in Newtown with renowned vegan Nan Sinclair, to laughing and teasing each other hand in hand down multiple red carpets, it was clear that they were besotted with one another.

Arabella was delighted that her plan was working out so well and Daisy was happily scrap booking all the positive media Garden and Bay was receiving. Daisy and Mack were doing such a great job of selling their new romance that even Daisy's family were convinced it was real.

Clem had called several times, begging for insider gossip on the 'Maisy' romance.

"Is he as hot in real life as he is on Home and Away?" she had asked rapturously, when she first found out. "Tell me what it's like to kiss him. Oh Daisy, tell me everything! Is his six-pack really as hard as it looks?"

"Eww! Clem! I am not answering any of those questions! As if I would tell you any of that, you are far too young to be having this conversation! Put Mum on!"

"I am not too young. Arabella tells me everything about all her hot clients, so there. MUM!"

Daisy laughed and held the phone away from her ear as Clem called out for Lola to come to come to the phone.

"Hang on, she's coming. She's just loading the car up for the naming ceremony for Ashanti and Bec's new baby. She made six cakes for some reason."

In the distance, Daisy could hear her mum calling out indignantly. "Clementine! You know I made six cakes so everyone could have some. There's a gluten-free banana bread, there's a vegan, gluten-free bundt, there's a sugar free flan, paleo brownies..."

A few moments later, Lola took the phone from her youngest daughter. "And most importantly, there is a full fat, full sugar chocolate cake just for me. So keep your hands to yourself Clementine...oh hello there darling! How is your hunky new bloke going?" she exclaimed a little breathlessly. "Tell me, is he really that good looking in real life?"

Daisy laughed. "Not you too Lola! I was going to tell you how much I missed you, but now I am hanging up in disgust. You're as bad as Clem! It's a good thing I love you both so much!"

The only dark spot seemed to be the absence of Royce

and Dan. Royce had returned from a trip to Darwin, only to instantly jet off again to cover an election in Thailand with less than a day's notice, despite promising to spend more time at home with Arabella. Although she wouldn't admit it, Arabella was missing him desperately.

Despite his surly behaviour, Daisy was also missing Dan and guiltily felt every single one of these beautifully orchestrated dates should have been with him. But she was also doing her best to keep Dan out of her mind. Their last encounter had left her feeling uneasy, and she was determined to stick to the pact they had made to cut off all contact for the full two weeks. It just felt easier that way.

The only activity she refused to do with Mack was surf.

"No Arabella, come on, that's me and Dan's thing. I don't want to share it with anyone, least of all Mack!" Daisy exclaimed, when Arabella broached the subject of doing an ad for Glass, a high fashion surf label that had scored Sylvia Holden as the new face of the label. Sylvia was the current number one surfer in the world now that the World Surf League had opened its competition to both male and female competitors and was going to feature in the new ad campaign alongside Belle Benson, one of Australia's top skaters and Marie Iluka, the triple gold medal winning swimming star from the last Olympics. Glass had asked Daisy to join them.

"Why on earth would they want me alongside such amazing sports stars?" continued Daisy, looking at photos of the other three sports stars strewn across the dining table.

"Well, because you are just as incredible," replied Arabella vaguely. "You have become a bit of a role model for healthy, empowered living, you know."

"I suppose having Mack on the side-lines doesn't hurt either right," replied Daisy drily.

Arabella looked sheepish. "Yeah, your faux-beau does have a little bit to do with it...but I promise you, the label is amazing and you will have a lot of fun! Here, have a look at their website."

Arabella was managing press for Glass, and she knew that Daisy would be impressed the label's commitment to marine conservation, using recycled plastic fibre in its clothing and contributing a percentage of its profits to the removal of plastic debris from the ocean.

She was right. As Daisy took Arabella's laptop and read more about the founders of Glass and their ethos and product development process, the more she became intrigued by the interesting duo who owned the label. Stu and Ben Harrison-Muller were two former pro-surfers, who had met at university on the Sunshine Coast, fallen in love and combined Ben's marine conservation work with Stu's fashion talent to create the eco-fashion label. They now lived in Noosa with their three adorable kids, Sasha, Molly and Tom, and two dogs, a Rottweiler named Artie and a fox terrier named Ivan. They had begrudgingly opened a small office in Sydney when the label had grown too big to be managed solely from Queensland, but had stubbornly refused to relocate the whole business, wanting to keep jobs in their hometown and stay as close to their favourite surf break as possible.

"Fine, I'll do it. These guys seem amazing. I would love to meet them!" said Daisy, eventually.

"I knew you would," replied Arabella with a relieved grin. "There will be plenty of time to chat with them at the shoot, but I will see if they want to have dinner afterwards so you can do some serious networking!"

———

The morning of the shoot dawned bright and clear. Arabella was thrilled to see the waves at Bondi small enough to be manageable, yet so clear they looked like polished glass. They set up the cameras on the north end of the beach, with some curtained change rooms for privacy from the growing throng surrounding the location shoot, as well as a convertible jeep and a stack of boards, oars, balls and other sporting goods to play with as props.

Royce's friend Terrence was directing the action. He made sure the morning was a lot of fun for Daisy, Sylvia, Belle and Marie, as they posed on the sand and in the water, showing off the beautiful swimwear and beach clothes that were built for strong, active women. Daisy was relieved to see the brand had a good selection of one-piece swimmers and rashies that would cover up her scars, and mentally thanked AB for her discretion.

"You surf right?" asked Sylvia, picking up a board and handing it over to Daisy. "You game for a bit of competition?"

Daisy burst out laughing. Sylvia was the best surfer in the world, and she was sure she would be outgunned at every wave. But Daisy had grown up surfing and was most at ease in the water, so she tucked the board under her arm.

"Sure thing world champ, I'll take you on!"

"Not without us you won't," added Belle with a grin, as she and Marie grabbed the remaining boards.

Whooping with the delight, the four women ran down the sand and hit the water, sliding easily onto the boards and paddling out onto the green-glass waves of North Bondi beach.

As Arabella, Stu and Ben stood on the beach watching, the four women began to compete, furiously and good-naturedly. The camera crew had quickly swapped over to their waterproof gear and had paddled out to capture the fun in the water and were rewarded with shot after amazing shot of the four women carving up Bondi's famous beach break.

———

Mack, who had been sitting in the shade of the jeep ignoring the shoot, looked up from his book in surprise.

"She's really good at this AB," he observed.

Arabella turned as Mack stood up, not taking his eyes off Daisy.

"Of course she is, she's incredible," Arabella replied, wondering what Mack was up to.

"She is! And this is exactly what we want Arabella!" exclaimed Stu in delight. "None of these pouty, overly sexualised swimwear models, we make clothes for real men and real women who want to take on the world!"

"Umm, honey, I think Arabella knows that since she read the brief and set up this shoot today," replied Ben, laughing gently at his husband's excitement and squeezing his arm affectionately.

Arabella smiled at Stu and Ben. "You guys are amazing, and you make beautiful clothes! I'm just so happy we could be a part of this today! You know, Daisy and I would love to have dinner with you later if you are staying in town tonight."

"We'd love to get to know Daisy more—she really is an impressive young lady. Let me check our schedule and we can chat more after the shoot," replied Ben with a grin.

———

Back on the beach after their impromptu surf competition, Sylvia high-fived Daisy and the others in appreciation.

"Wow, ladies, you're not too bad, you know that!" she laughed. "I may have to watch myself next year—any of you could steal my crown!"

Mack, who had been watching Daisy carving it up with the world champion in surprise, walked over to where she was drying herself off. For a moment he stood looking down at her, his eyes speculative and admiring. "Daisy Gardiner, you are a fucking delight, do you know that?" he said, before wrapping her up in the towel and lifting her off her feet for a long, spine-tingling, toe-curling kiss. The three other women good naturedly wolf-whistled at Mack and Daisy, while the cameras clicked frantically, and the assembled crowd cheered. But Daisy could no longer hear anything, her ears were so full of her own beating heart, as Mack's soft lips covered hers, searching and probing deeper. She forgot she was meant to be playing a role and melted into Mack's kiss, wrapping her arms around his neck and losing herself in his soft touch.

———

As things on the beach settled down and the camera crew packed up their gear, Daisy sat down on the sand with Stu and Ben for a chat.

"Thanks for being part of the shoot today, Daisy," Ben said.

"Oh you guys, it's been an absolute pleasure! I love your clothes, the way you make them is so special. Plus also, it's not often I get to surf with women like that, so I've had an amazing day!"

"Arabella tells us you're from Byron, like her. We love Byron...we've spent Christmas there a few times with our friends Rohan and Celeste Walden. Do you know them?"

"Oh yes! Not really well, but everyone knows Celeste, and Rohan was one of my sister's teachers at school. Celeste comes by my market stall a bit actually, she is one of my best customers!"

"Yes, we have heard a lot about Garden and Bay from Celeste. I didn't put two and two together until we were talking to Mack and Arabella this week," replied Stu. "You've done a great job with it and we're always excited to hear about socially conscious fashion. We'd love to hear more about your products from Fiji!"

As Daisy told them about her work and the fabric manufactures in the Pacific Islands, her love for textiles and traditional production methods lit up her face and she grew more and more animated. The two men smiled and exchanged knowing looks.

"So now I am at a crossroads," she finished. "Not sure where to next, but I am pretty sure that this is the end of the line for me with the shop. Time for a new adventure."

"Listen Daisy, we have to get back to Noosa. Molly has

a school play tonight, and we did the costumes, and she will kill us if we are not there for it. But we will be back on Sunday for the White party—we have some pieces in the show," said Stu.

"Can we catch up, then? We would really like to talk to you about all this more. We'll have more time after the show on Sunday," added Ben, getting up and dusting the sand off his board shorts.

"Of course!" replied Daisy. "I'd love to. It's been really great meeting you guys!"

TEN

Oh-Em-G *Squee!!! Click here to see the Oh-Em-G exclusive photos of Mack and Daisy smooching up a storm on Bondi Beach! 'Maisy' is in love, and we are here for it!*

———

As the week slid by, Daisy was surprised to realise she was having a lot of fun. Speaking with Stu and Ben about their business and the opportunities of ethical fashion had inspired her, reigniting her love of design. Her mind was whirling with interesting ideas for new fabrics and styles. Daisy was so inspired that she had started carrying around a notebook and had been staying up late sketching out ideas and researching different production factories.

Daisy also realised that despite her initial misgivings, Mack was turning out to be not quite as bad as she had initially thought. In fact, he had been good company, and they had been having a great time hanging out together. She had relaxed around him, and she had discovered that he could be sweet and funny when he wasn't putting on a show for the paparazzi or for the many fans flocking to his side for autographs, making her laugh uproariously at his unpredictable and witty jokes. Daisy knew he was a great actor, but part of her was wondering if they did actually have a connection. Perhaps she had been very wrong about him? She thought back to that kiss on the beach, the one time he had kissed her properly, and she shivered in delight, her stomach fizzing at the thought of those lips touching her again. Clearly, they had chemistry. But was it real?

———

Two days after the Glass shoot, the producers of Home and Away had arranged for a cocktail party on a yacht on Sydney Harbour, as a farewell party for Mack. Although he had filmed his last scene several months ago, his character Charlie was only just leaving the show this week and the show's public relations team was going all out on the publicity stunts.

Mack, Daisy and Arabella were being driven to Darling Harbour by a hired car service. It was a lot of fun being so dressed up in the back of such a fancy ride. Arabella was wearing a strapless navy jumpsuit, patterned with sailing boats. A white chiffon headscarf, ala Grace Kelly, oversized sunglasses and flat navy sandals completed her look. Daisy had chosen a simple white dress, with off the shoulder bell sleeves and gold sandals, which she was now regretting, having left her sunscreen at home.

Even Mack, who would look drop dead sexy in a garbage bag, was dressed up for the occasion and Daisy was trying hard not to notice how sexy he looked. He was wearing white shorts, held tight around his waist by a navy and white striped belt. His striped blue and white dress shirt was rolled up to his elbows, and he had on matching navy boat shoes. It was a little bit preppy for Mack—he tended towards a more 'grungy, just rolled out of bed' look, but Daisy thought he looked charming.

Mack, on the other hand, was looking down at himself scowling. "Why are you looking at me, Daisy?" he snapped. "These clothes are ridiculous."

Daisy flushed, thinking she had been caught checking out her faux beau.

"You look fine," she replied, frantically opening her bag and looking for her sketch book to keep her eyes away from Mack's cranky glare.

"I look like a prat," he replied petulantly. "Stupid stylists."

He pulled out the paperback he seemed to carry around wherever he went and refused to speak for the rest of the car ride.

Arabella sighed as she looked from Daisy to Mack, both of them studiously avoiding each other.

Was Royce right? Was her job really just about babysitting spoilt celebrities?

———

Daisy was still drawing in her notebook when their car pulled up to Darling Harbour. The entertainment precinct was full of people and already Daisy could tell it was going to be much noisier outside of the car. It took her a moment to realise that the screaming and cheers were actually for them, or rather, for Mack. She looked up in surprise to see the car surrounded by a horde of excited teenagers.

She looked around at Arabella and Mack in alarm.

"Are you kidding me? We have to go out there?" she asked, gesturing at the surging sea of adolescents pushing up against the town car.

"It's fine. The security team will clear a path for us. But you have to put your sketch pad away. Why don't you leave it here in the car? You won't need it out on the water, trust me." Arabella unzipped a large tote bag and gestured for Daisy to stow her art supplies. But Mack shook his head.

"No, it's ok AB. I'll carry Daisy's bag. She has been so struck by inspiration lately I think she'd start drawing on the deck if she didn't have her paper!" He turned and winked at Daisy, clearly over his earlier bad mood, before taking her bag and slinging it over his shoulder. "Alright then ladies, let's be famous!"

Daisy watched in awe as Mack stepped out of the car, grinning at the crowd. He stopped to shake hands and kiss one lucky girl's cheek. The young girl swooned and started crying, and for a second, Daisy found herself jealous of the attention Mack was paying to all the fans. But as if reading her thoughts, he stopped and turned back, and held out his hand to her.

Arabella pushed Daisy gently from behind. "Go, get out there! You have to walk with him!" she hissed, making sure Daisy's outfit was camera ready.

Daisy stepped out of the car and grabbed on to Mack's hand gratefully. Although Daisy had experienced several celebrity events in the last week, this was certainly the most high profile. The combination of the noise and closeness of the screaming crowd and the incessant flashes of the paparazzi, who were waiting for them on the other side of the roped off area, was overwhelming. Mack squeezed her hand tightly and leant down to kiss her cheek.

"It's ok, I'll look out for you," he whispered, before straightening up and smiling at the crowd again.

"Isn't she beautiful?" he called out over the din. "I'm a lucky guy!"

The crowd went wild at their brief moment of affection.

Mack and Daisy, followed closely by Arabella, moved on down the red carpet, towards to the yacht. They stopped and posed for some photos on the jetty before thankfully walking up the gangway and onto the boat.

It was only when they were on board and Daisy had time to look back and see the crowd from above that it dawned on her just how famous Mack was. She hadn't watched Home and Away in years, but Arabella had filled her in on Mack's storyline. Mack's character Charlie had started off as the show's resident bad boy. He had arrived in Summer Bay looking to get revenge on Lisa, his high school sweetheart, for breaking his heart many years ago. But when he finally tracked her down, he found out that Lisa had fallen pregnant 15 years ago and, knowing that Charlie wasn't ready to be a father, she had panicked and fled to Summer Bay.

Desperate to win back Lisa and get to know the daughter he never knew he had, Charlie had changed his ways and for a moment it looked like Lisa and Charlie and their daughter Grace were going to live happily ever after.

But tragedy struck and Lisa was diagnosed with a rare, incurable disease, dying just one day after she and Charlie had gotten married on the beach at sunset. Determined to make a proper life for himself and Grace, Charlie had decided to leave Summer Bay and take Grace to Brisbane, where his parents lived, to start over.

The Harbour cruise had been planned by the show's PR team as a farewell to Mack and Malia, the actress who played Grace, as they were both leaving the show. They were also celebrating Malia's upcoming sixteenth birthday. It was no coincidence that such a high profile public party was taking place the same week as Mack and Malia's last episode.

Once all the Home and Away stars and producers and a gaggle of very lucky reporters from TV Week and Girlfriend magazine were safely on board, the boat slowly made its way out into the harbour. Several security boats followed them to make sure that the paparazzi, following in hot pursuit, were kept at a safe, yet photographable distance at all times.

Daisy and Arabella stood under the covered deck next to the buffet, watching the formalities. Mack, Malia and their co-stars assembled for a photo shoot, using the Harbour Bridge and Opera House as a backdrop. As the yacht meandered its way past Fort Dennison and Garden Island, and around the ritzy harbour-side suburbs of Point Piper and Rose Bay, Daisy listened to the speeches, laughing affectionately at the hilarious anecdotes of Mack's time on set in Summer Bay.

Carol, one of the senior producers on the show, stepped up to the microphone. "Like Charlie, Mack Boddington has been nothing but trouble since the first day he set foot on set," she began. "There have definitely been days where we would wonder if we made the right choice casting him. But like Charlie, Mack has also kept us laughing, and has made us all love him unreservedly over the last few years. Like Charlie, Mack has become family. We have watched this young guy grow and mature as an actor, and as a man, and we couldn't be happier for him he has been given this opportunity to take this next exciting step in his career and his life."

Carol looked down at Mack fondly. "Thank you for keeping life interesting, Mack. We will miss you!"

She gestured to Mack to join her on the small makeshift stage. They hugged, and Mack sniffed dramatically into the microphone.

"Thanks for making me cry in front of the cast and crew, Carol! Now I really need to leave the country!" The crowd laughed appreciatively.

"But seriously, I know I've been a bit of wild card over the last few years, and I can't thank Carol and the other producers enough for their continuing trust and support. I've learnt so much in my time here and there have been many people who have helped me grow up and want to be a better man." Mack paused and searched out Daisy in the crowd. "There are people here today that mean more to me than they know, and I just want to say thank you to all the amazing actors I've worked with, the patient and talented crew who make this show come to life and the directors who have helped me grow professionally and personally over these last few years. I know I haven't always been the best I could be, but I want to tell you all that I won't waste this opportunity. I know how lucky I am, and I am going to make every second of this new adventure count. But I will miss you all terribly though! Thanks and I promise you I will send you all autographed headshots from Hollywood!"

The crowd laughed again as Mack theatrically air-kissed the crowd and stepped down, signalling the end of the formalities.

After the toasts had ended and the crowd dispersed, Mack and Malia made their way over to Daisy and Arabella.

"Marls, this is my friend Daisy and my publicist Arabella. Ladies, this is the awesome Malia Salinger. We've been working together for two years and let me tell you, this kid is the best damn actor I've ever seen. I don't know why she wants to give it all away...such a waste of raw talent!"

Mack put his arm around Malia and hugged her affectionately. In return, Malia grinned and pinched his arm hard.

"This guy is such a jerk!" she laughed, smiling up at Mack. "Lucky I love him like the big brother I never wanted!"

"I'm kidding! You are crazy smart, kiddo, and you are going to do amazing things." Mack turned to Daisy and Arabella. "I am very proud of her," he said with a genuine smile.

"So what are you going to do now?" asked Arabella.

"Actually, I'm going to go to uni to study engineering," Malia explained. "I've been accepted into an early entry Aerospace program at Sydney University, so I just need to finish year 12 with good marks and I'm in. The show has been so much fun, but it's not what I planned to do forever. Now I have enough money saved up that I can pay for my degree straight up and not have to work while I'm studying. Mack and my parents think I should splurge a little, maybe go on a holiday, but I've got to keep my grades up!"

Malia stopped talking and looked across at the buffet.

"Ooh, they have sliders! That's the other great thing about not being on tv any more...I can eat whatever I like and not worry about it!"

Daisy and Arabella laughed as Malia filled a plate with mini burgers and curly fries.

"Wow! That is so cool!" replied Daisy. "I didn't go to uni. I wanted to, but life had other plans for me. Tell me what sort of things you'll be studying...is it aircraft engineering or space engineering?"

Daisy also filled a plate of food and joined Malia at one of the small tables on the back deck, listening as Malia explained the space program she would start next year. Daisy was so engrossed in Malia's plans that she didn't notice that Mack had disappeared until he was standing next to them, holding her satchel, which was now bulging with bottles and containers of food.

"Hey Marls, do you mind if I steal Daisy? I need to get away from all this craziness for a bit."

Malia stood up and threw her arms around Mack's waist. "Yeah, I understand. Just be good to this one. She is really different. And you'll be at my real birthday tomorrow, right?"

"Of course I'll be at your real birthday tomorrow. I wouldn't miss it for the world."

Malia turned to Daisy.

"Would you like to come to my party as well?" she

asked, a little shyly. "It's at Luna Park! Please say yes, it would be so great if you could come with Mack!"

"I would love to! Thanks for the invitation!"

"It's been really nice meeting you Daisy!" Malia leant forward to give Daisy a hug and whispered in her ear.

"I promise he is not as bad as he pretends to be. If you give him a chance, he is the best guy in the world."

Taking hold of Daisy's hand, Mack quietly led her down to the bottom deck, away from the rest of the party and out of view of the paparazzi boats lined up on the other side of the yacht.

"What's going on Mack?" Daisy asked suspiciously, as they reached the bottom of the stairs.

Mack looked around furtively and stopped in front of a small dinghy, one of the ship's lifeboats. He quickly lowered the satchel over the side and onto the seat, next to an esky and several large bottles of water.

"We have been cooped up for far too long, Gardenia. We have been performing monkeys all day, all week, and we need a break. We are staging a jailbreak!" Mack started climbing over the edge of the yacht, but Daisy grabbed his arm and pulled him back.

"Are you kidding? We can't steal a boat! And we can't leave AB here alone!"

"We are not stealing the boat, we are borrowing it. I've already hired it from the captain. Arabella will be fine. Malia will keep her company."

Mack stopped and looked at Daisy and arched his eyebrow suggestively, before smiling his megawatt celebrity smile at her.

"Urgh," she groaned, climbing over the edge of the boat. "I hate it when you do that!"

"Works every time," Mack laughed, following closely behind.

As soon as they had cast off from the yacht and were safely out of shouting range, Mack dialled Arabella's mobile.

Daisy could just make out her best friend back on the boat, answering her phone and looking around wildly.

"Hey PR queen. Just letting you know I've kidnapped Daisy and I am taking her away for the afternoon. We need some time out. Don't come looking for us! I promise I'll have her home by curfew!"

Daisy laughed as she watched Arabella turn and gaze out over the harbour until she spotted them in the dingy. She waved merrily as Arabella shook her head in resignation and turned back to the party.

"So, where are we going?" asked Daisy, as Mack gunned the engine and turned the small boat north.

"There is this little bay up near the Quarantine Station, called Store Beach. You can only get there by boat. You'll love it."

Daisy settled back in the boat, enjoying the cool harbour breeze and the splash of salt spray over her face. For the first time in days, she felt free.

This was a great idea, she thought happily as the boat bounced along in the wake of the Manly ferry.

Soon they had passed over the choppy water where Sydney Harbour opens up into the Tasman Sea and headed towards the cliffs of North Head. Mack slowed the boat and let it drift gently into a small, secluded cove. It was completely empty.

"I didn't realise you were such an accomplished sailor, Mack," Daisy laughed, after he had anchored the dinghy to a large piece of driftwood.

"Oh Gardenia, I am full of surprises. Actually, I grew up not far from here. Sailing runs in the family."

They set up camp under the shade of a small grove of casuarina trees and sat in silence, taking in the stillness of their private beach. After a while, Mack lay back on the blanket and opened up a book, while Daisy got out her sketch pad and set to work. She glanced over at him occasionally.

"What are you reading this week, Mack?" she asked, curiosity finally getting the better of her.

Mack looked up from his book. "Would you believe The Old Man and the Sea? I thought it was rather fitting for a day on the harbour."

Daisy laughed and returned to her sketching.

They stayed like this for well over an hour, comfortably lost in their own worlds, until Mack sat up and gazed out over the bay.

"Look at the colour of that water, Daisy. Come on, we should swim before the sun goes down and it gets too cold." He stood up, pulling her up with him.

Daisy looked out over the turquoise bay. It was so inviting. She shivered in delight at the thought of plunging into the cool, clear water. There was just one problem. "I don't have any swimmers."

"Can't you swim in your underwear? I'm just going to wear my shorts."

Daisy turned to Mack and gestured at her outfit. "Umm, look at this dress. There's no substantial underwear under this!"

"Really," breathed Mack, his eyes narrowing as he jokingly leered down Daisy's top. "I stand by my original plan. Swim in your underwear!"

"Stop it!" Daisy laughed, punching him in the arm.

"Ok, you can have my shirt. It'll probably be a bit see through, but I promise not to look."

Daisy's heart flip-flopped as Mack untucked his shirt and unbuttoned it before peeling it off and tossing it to her. Surely it was illegal for anyone to look this good?

"Please turn around," she said, turning away from Mack so she could slip out of her dress and into the shirt.

"Yes, Ma'am!" he laughed, turning slightly away but still glancing over his shoulder when he thought she wasn't looking.

"Stop looking Mack! I can hear you looking!"

"I wasn't! I promise!"

Daisy finished buttoning up the shirt and turned back to glare at Mack in mock annoyance.

Suddenly she grinned, a mischievous plan hatching in her mind.

"Last one in's a rotten egg!"

She pushed him backwards, taking him by surprise, and ran down the beach. Mack stumbled a few steps, giving her a head start, but by the time she reached the water's edge, he had caught up to her. He scooped her up in his arms and carried her out into the deeper water. She screamed with laugher as he plunged them both down into the cool depths, his arms holding her tight against him. They quickly surfaced, gasping for air, laughing and splashing each other like kids.

When they were worn out from that game, they floated amiably in the shallows next to one another, their fingertips brushing now and then, causing bottle after bottle of champagne to pop in Daisy's belly, bubbling and fizzing in the most delicious way.

"Did you know that there is a colony of fairy penguins that live near this beach?" asked Mack, on the third time they had lazily floated past each other.

"Really? That is so cool! Where are they now?"

"They are out to sea at the moment, but they will come back in when the weather gets colder to lay their eggs for the season. Penguins mate for life and always come back to the same beach, year after year. I like that about them," Mack explained.

"How do you know all this?" Daisy asked, as Mack drifted by again.

"Told you I'm full of surprises," he laughed, before drifting away again.

After a while, Mack sat up in the water and caught Daisy's wrist and pulled her to him.

"Why do you have a scar on your stomach?" he asked roughly. "What happened? Did someone hurt you?"

Daisy blushed and pulled Mack's shirt down, unconsciously wrapping her arms around her stomach.

"You're really uncomfortable about it, aren't you? I'm sorry. I just...it looks really bad and I don't like the thought of someone hurting you."

Daisy looked up at Mack and saw genuine concern in his eyes.

She sighed and relaxed a little.

"When I finished high school, Mum and I were in a bad car accident. I had a lot of internal injuries and had to have a pin put in my hip. My parents were really amazing. My mum couldn't work for ages and she had to look after me and they had to take out a second mortgage to pay for all the hospital bills."

Daisy stopped and took a deep breath. "I have felt really guilty about it for so many years. I didn't go to uni. I stayed home so that I could help them out financially, but they ended up helping me out again when I started the shop. I feel like I've never been able to give them back what they deserve. They are the best parents. That's why I'm thinking of selling Garden and Bay to Thread Bare. Because I need to pay them back. I want them to have the kind of life they were always planning for. That's part of why I am doing all this now."

Mack didn't say anything, but he reached out to take hold of Daisy's hand, squeezing it tightly.

"But I also have all these ideas about what I want to do. I'm not sure I want to sell the shop, but I really need to do it if I want to do anything new."

"So what do you want to do?" he asked.

"Ever since the Glass shoot, I have been having all these ideas about how to produce sustainable materials, and how to do it in a way that supports traditional crafts people...like what Rise Beyond the Reef does, just scalable and sustainable. I need to sit down and work it all out."

Mack watched Daisy as she spoke, smiling gently as she became more and more animated.

"What are you waiting for then? Go and do it."

Daisy started to protest, but Mack interrupted her. "Daisy, seriously. You are really smart. And as long as you are alive and healthy and in a position to, you should do something good."

Mack looked away, his eyes darkening for a moment. "When I was a kid, about 15, my little sister died. She had bone cancer. She was eleven."

"That's why you chose CMRI for the Bay to Beach run?" asked Daisy, squeezing his hand back.

Mack nodded. "When Tess died it was really hard. She was so sure she was going to get better; I think she had me convinced. I wasn't prepared for it when it happened. She was going to be a doctor. A paediatric doctor so she could help kids like her. She always said that as long as we wanted to change the world, we could change the world." Mack paused for a while, lost in his own thoughts. "We should probably get out and dry off, so we can get back before dark," he said finally, noticing the setting sun. He looked down at Daisy and smiled.

"Hey, it's been fun hanging out today. I really enjoyed it."

"Yeah, it was a great idea. Thanks for kidnapping me!"

They quickly packed up and set off for Darling Harbour. Daisy was grateful that they'd had the small cove to themselves all afternoon. The harbour was less busy in the middle of the week than it would have been on a weekend. The sun was sitting low in the west as they rounded Bradley's Head, heading towards the Harbour Bridge and Darling Harbour. It was getting cool in the fading light and Daisy shivered.

Mack bent forward from his spot at the back of the

boat. Still holding on to the outboard motor, he rummaged through the bag and pulled out the picnic blanket. He tossed it to Daisy with a grin. "Wrap up in this and come and sit here with me," he said, gesturing to the seat next to him.

Daisy gratefully took the blanket and moved back one seat. Mack reached around with his spare arm and pulled her close. She rested her head on his shoulder and watched the fiery sunset glowing behind the bridge.

She couldn't think of a more perfect afternoon.

———

Arabella was in bed by the time Daisy got home, having left a note stuck to her bedroom door.

Traitor! it read. *But hope you guys had fun!*

Still smiling from the Arabella's note and the all-round fun day she and Mack had had, Daisy had a shower and got into bed.

But the second she lay down, Mack's words came back to her.

"So, what do you want to do?"

"What are you waiting for? Go and do it."

Daisy sat up and reached for her sketch pad. Suddenly, she knew what she had to do. She wanted to work for a company like Glass. She wanted to focus on sourcing sustainable materials and fabrics. She wanted to keep learning about different production techniques from around the world and she wanted to find ways to support communities that were losing their traditional artisans. As she looked at her notes and designs, it all fell into place, so she took out her computer and began typing madly.

Once she had completed the proposal, she sat back and thought for a moment. Mack's words kept echoing in her mind.

Go and do it.

Daisy proofread the document one last time. Taking a deep breath, she pressed send.

It's done, she thought, with an exhilarated grin. *I have taken back control of my life.*

There was no way she could sleep now. She was too excited about her idea and felt like she needed to keep going, keep sorting out her life.

She looked at her watch. It was only 12.25am. Not too late to go knocking on someone's door.

Dressing quickly in the first clothes she could find, Daisy quietly slipped out of the apartment and pedalled quickly down to Hall Street and around the bend to Forest Knoll Avenue. She wasn't sure what was going to happen when she got there, but she had a feeling that she needed to see Dan sooner, rather than later, to figure out what he really meant to her.

As she stood on the familiar balcony, her stomach twisted nervously. She heard Costello scratching along the floorboards and Dan's familiar footsteps following along behind. The door opened and Dan looked out sleepily.

For a moment he stood silent, looking at her, a little confused. After a minute, he rubbed his eyes and laughed.

"Daisy, what the hell are you wearing?"

Daisy looked down. She had to admit, of all the crazy outfits she'd thrown together, this was the strangest. Her denim cut-off shorts were fine, and in the right circum-stances, Arabella's red cowboy boots probably would look fine. But worn with her rashie? Daisy started to laugh, too. Nope. That was not a good look.

"Hi Dan," she said, when she had caught her breath.

"Come in. I'll put the kettle on and make some tea."

She followed Dan into the kitchen. "So how are you?" she asked.

Dan fumbled with his phone for a moment, before switching it off and turning around to face Daisy.

"I've had a shitty week. My girlfriend has been traipsing around with some dickhead and I've been made redundant from the job I've had for almost eight years."

Dan pushed some papers across the bench towards Daisy. She scanned the cover letter. The council had undergone a restructure and Dan's unit had been merged into another team. Staff from both teams had to be let go in order to save money.

"But I don't understand? You've been there for so long! How can they only tell you about this now?"

"It's been in the pipeline for a while, but I didn't think it would happen so fast. And I get the feeling they didn't like all the unwanted attention I've been getting over the last few weeks. Yeah, so you know, without a job, I could lose everything. It's not cheap living here in Bondi. So while you have been living the highlife with...that guy...I've been here desperately trying to figure out how to keep myself afloat."

"I'm really sorry Dan," said Daisy, feeling terrible about the predicament he was in, but also feeling uneasy about his surly attitude and eagerness to blame everyone but himself for his bad luck. She wasn't the reason he'd been let go. She thought back to the last few times she had seen him. With a sinking heart, she realised Arabella had pegged him right from the start.

"Distract me then. What's new with you and your famous boyfriend? Are you engaged yet?" Dan joked half-heartedly.

Daisy frowned for a moment, then pushed her uneasiness aside.

"Well, it's nearly over, thank goodness. I'm still not sure what I'll do, but I actually had this idea." She stopped and looked at Dan, her face lighting up as she started explaining the proposal she just put together.

"I met these really awesome fashion designers from Queensland. They have a sustainable surf label, and they want to make it 100% recycled and repurposed. I've asked them if they want to buy a share in Garden and Bay, make it a sub-brand of Glass. And I want to work with them, managing their fair trade and textile development."

Daisy stopped and looked at Dan, excited to be sharing her idea with someone.

But Dan shook his head. "I don't know Daisy; it sounds like a huge risk. I mean, you've never really done this before, have you? What do you know about this business? I think it's really risky."

"Oh, I, umm..." Daisy was puzzled. Why was he being so negative about her idea?

"Actually, this is building on the work I have been doing with my shop in Byron. I kind of already do this work, just on a smaller scale."

"Look, I just don't think this kind of thing is going to

work. I don't think you thought this through. Have you told your boyfriend, Mack? What did he think about it? Did he tell you it was a good idea?"

Dan's tone was sullen and angry, and Daisy was taken aback by his strong reaction to her news.

Suddenly, Dan walked over to where Daisy was standing, oblivious to her shocked reaction, and put his arms around her.

"I'm sorry. We shouldn't be talking about stuff like this when we've been apart for so long. Come outside and let's forget all about that and get re-acquainted."

Dan took Daisy's arm and pulled her gently out on to the veranda, where he started kissing the side of her neck. He slid one hand down her back to pull her close to him and reached his other hand up under her shirt, lifting the fabric up so her bare skin was pressed up against his.

But Daisy pushed him away angrily.

"Dan! Stop! What are you doing?"

Dan pulled away and looked at her, confused. "What do you mean? Don't you want to? I mean, isn't that why you came over?" he asked, still breathing heavily.

"No! I came over because I missed you and I wanted to talk! I'm sorry, this is all a bit full on. I don't really know what to think."

"I can't believe you are being such a bitch about this," Dan said coldly, crossing his arms defensively.

Daisy looked at him sadly, and in that instant, she knew it was over.

"I am so sorry that I have hurt you. But this is over Dan. It's really nothing to do with Mack. You are just not the person I thought you were."

Without looking back, Daisy turned and walked out of the house, into the cool night air. She stopped to catch her breath at the front gate, listening to see if he was following her.

He wasn't.

So that's done, Daisy thought as she got on to her bike and started pedalling home, expecting to cry.

But all she felt was relief.

Eleven

———

The following day, Daisy woke up with mixed feelings. She knew she had made the right choice and that her relationship with Dan was over. He really wasn't the guy she thought he was. Arabella had known. There was something not quite right about him. On the other hand, although she knew she had made the right decision to end things with Dan, Daisy was still feeling stung by his reaction to her proposal and how stupid he had made her feel. Even in the light of day, his reaction was making her second guess her email to Ben and Stu.

What if I have made a huge mistake and end up looking really stupid? she thought to herself, as she lay in bed staring up at the ceiling, her stomach roiling with nerves.

But instead of dwelling on the unpleasantness of the night before, Daisy decided to throw herself into getting ready for Malia's party. She forced herself out of bed and into the shower. She was looking forward to seeing Mack again, and she smiled as she thought back to their afternoon at Store Beach yesterday. Daisy also wanted to stop and get Malia a present on the way, and she had seen just the thing at a small gift shop on Hall Street.

But first, she thought to herself ten minutes later, staring into her wardrobe and weighing up her options, *what do you wear to a famous actress/aspiring aero-engineer's 16th birthday at Luna Park?*

After pulling her entire wardrobe to pieces, Daisy finally settled on a pair of skinny boyfriend jeans and a blush pink cotton blouse with a thick embroidered silver yoke collar that ran all the way down towards her belly button. Her brown sandals and brown satchel, and a pair of beaded and fringed earrings, completed her look. Once she was satisfied, she said farewell to Arabella and set off for a day at the funfair.

Mack was waiting for her at the ferry wharf in front of Luna Park's famous grinning clown face. He was wearing dark sunnies and had a baseball cap pulled down over his face and was leaning against the railing looking out over the water. Daisy spotted him as soon as she stepped off the ferry and smiled. Even covered up and from a distance, he was unmistakably Mack Boddington. As usual, he had a book in hand and was too engrossed in the story to notice that she had walked up beside him.

"Excuse me, do I know you?" she joked, nudging him gently in the ribs. "You look awfully like this guy who kidnapped me and held me hostage on a deserted beach this one time."

Mack turned to her and smiled.

"Oh yes, you look familiar as well. You look like this girl I helped to liberate from our mutual PR overlords, who came on a fun afternoon out with me and had the time of her life," he drawled in reply.

"The time of her life? Really?"

Tucking the book in his back pocket, Mack leant forward and kissed Daisy on the cheek.

"You look really nice," he said, holding out his arm. "Shall we?"

Inside the park, they met up with Malia and her friends at the ticket booth and were soon ready for action. Far from being a celebrity party, this was a celebration reserved for her closest friends and family. Malia introduced Daisy to her parents, Dave and Sally, and her little sister Jasmine and unwrapped Daisy's present on the spot, exclaiming in delight at the build your own scale model of the Apollo 11 space craft.

"Thank you, Daisy! This is awesome! I can't wait to get home and start putting it together!" She hugged Daisy before dashing off to join her friends in the queue for the first ride.

Mack and Daisy followed Malia and her guests on ride after ride, shrieking with terrified laughter as they were dropped and flung and twirled by the rattly old rollercoasters. Mack was a hit with the younger crowd, not just because he was a handsome tv star but because he was actually really great at talking to Malia's friends. Daisy watched him laughing and gently teasing a group of Malia's old school friends, and she was pleasantly surprised when she saw him go out of his way to make sure one particularly shy young girl felt comfortable and included. He did the same with Malia's little sister, Jasmine, pushing her wheelchair to the front of each queue and making sure he was her personal escort up onto each of the rides, much to Jasmine's delight. This was yet another side to Mack that Daisy hadn't seen before.

He really is a surprising man, she thought affectionately, watching him laugh and play around with Malia and her friends.

After Dan's rudeness the night before, Daisy was reluctant to tell Mack about her proposal to Glass, despite desperately wanting to know what he thought. He was the inspiration for her action, after all. She was thankful the party was so busy that there was no chance to talk.

Soon Malia and her friends had ridden on all the rides several times over and were sitting at the café, exhausted and ready to go home.

"Yesterday was heaps of fun," said Daisy, as Mack brought her a stick of bright pink fairy floss. "But I think this has been the best part of the week."

"I agree. But there is one ride we haven't been on yet," said Mack, gesturing up at the ferris wheel. "I bet the view is amazing from up there once it gets darker. Should we do it...just one more?"

After saying their farewells to Malia and her family,

Mack and Daisy lined up for a sunset ride on the old ferris wheel. Sitting on top twenty minutes later, Daisy was finally alone with Mack for the first time since they had met at the ferry wharf that morning. Daisy looked at Mack, his arm draped casually across her shoulder and his gorgeous blue eyes twinkling in the warm sunset light. She realised with a start that she really liked him. Perhaps more than just liked him.

Does this make me the shallowest person in the world? Was Dan right? Have I just fallen for this guy because he is the most ridiculously good-looking guy I've ever seen? Did I give up on Dan too soon?

She pushed her guilty thoughts away. *No, Dan is not who I thought he was. There is something mean about him. Mack, on the other hand, is secretly the kindest guy I've ever met. How did I get them so mixed up?*

"Did you think any more about what we talked about yesterday?" asked Mack, breaking into her thoughts.

"Yeah, I did actually." Daisy reluctantly told him about the proposal she sent Ben and Stu. "I mean, I think it's an ok idea. I probably should have waited a bit, done some more research. It's probably not what they are looking for, and they'll probably laugh at me for it."

Mack looked at her quizzically. "Why would you think that? It sounds great and they are already super impressed by you. I think it sounds like a brilliant plan—it's a great solution for you because it gives you security to grow and learn, without having to give up Garden and Bay and fills a gap in Glass that Ben and Stu have already identified as something they need to look at. It's bloody clever. I'm super proud of you for seizing the day."

Daisy looked up at Mack shyly. "Really? Actually, you were my inspiration. After our chat yesterday. I kept thinking about what you said, so I just went and did it. Well, at least I've put it out there."

Mack was silent for a moment, staring at the blazing sunset. "Daisy, I've never met anyone like you," Mack said, trailing off for a moment. "I don't know what it is, but everything seems to be ok when I'm with you."

Daisy shivered in delight at his words. But she knew she had to be honest with him.

"Mack, listen. I'm not very good at this stuff. Back when I had the crash, I had this boyfriend, Jordan. We'd been together in high school, and we were both leaving for uni that week. But then the crash happened, and everything changed. I was really hurt, and he didn't come and see me for ages. When he did, it was to break up with me before he left for uni."

Daisy paused and closed her eyes, as the memories came flooding back. "At first, I thought it was because he felt guilty because he left me at the party. That's why Mum was driving me home. But when he broke up with me, he told me it was because he thought all my cuts and stitches were gross and he couldn't bring himself to touch me anymore. He said he thought I looked like some kind of lab experiment gone bad. I know I have recovered, and I want to be a huge champion of body positivity but sometimes I just feel like that gross, broken girl and I get nervous. I guess deep down I don't know how anyone could really like me, after all that. I've had a couple of relationships since, but none of them have been very serious. I never really let them go too far."

Daisy stopped talking and took a deep breath, before looking up at Mack shyly. "I like you, Mack. I've really had fun these last few days. But please don't string me along. I don't want that sort of relationship, ok."

Mack's arm around her tightened around her as she spoke. "I know," he whispered into her hair, as he gently kissed the top of her head. "I know." He looked down at her, his blue eyes fierce and tender. "I'm not going to hurt you, I promise."

"Just so you know, I think you are so cool," he continued. "I'm sorry you were hurt, but I don't think you'd be you without the experiences you've had. You are amazing and you are beautiful. And I'm going to show the world just how great you are."

Mack pulled out his phone and leant down to take a selfie of them kissing. But instead of a kiss, he blew a raspberry onto her cheek, and she burst out laughing. The photo was beautiful—candid and tender. It was no surprise that it went viral in a matter of hours.

"You know what, I think I have seriously underestimated you, Mack Boddington. You are not so bad after all," Daisy said, with a grin.

Mack arched his eyebrows wickedly. "Oh, really?" he asked, leaning forward to brush his lips against Daisy's cheek and ear and neck. She shivered with each soft touch until she could take it no more and reached out to pull his face to hers, their lips meeting as they breathlessly dissolved into each other.

Before them, the sun slipped over the horizon and the lights of Sydney city blinkered on. A cruise ship blasted its mournful farewell as it left Circular Quay. But Mack and Daisy were too lost in each other to notice.

TWELVE

@**ReturnoftheMack** *Isn't she the loveliest?*

———

"Hey Gardiner, you know I am going to beat you, right?"

"In your dreams, Boddington, in your dreams!"

"You're in my dreams every night baby...but I'm still gonna beat you!"

"Not if you don't choke on your own corny jokes first!"

Daisy and Mack were at the starting line of the Bay to Beach fun run, shoving and jostling each other playfully as they prepared to run the eight kilometres from Rushcutters Bay to Bondi. Around them, excited onlookers took photos, while a gaggle of star struck teens were waving glittery posters from the side-lines.

Go Mack! they read. *We love you!*

Suddenly the starting gun went off. Daisy pushed Mack to the side with a triumphant laugh and dashed out into an early lead. Mack quickly caught up and ran circles around her a few times before surging forward to take a slight lead.

"How on earth are you this in shape with all that hard partying you usually do!" gasped Daisy, as she caught up to him and they took on the steep hill past Edgecliff Station side by side.

"It's because I've been so busy running after you, haven't you noticed?" Mack panted back.

Daisy rolled her eyes and pushed forward, with Mack in hot pursuit. Together, they bickered and jostled each other as they easily ran the relatively short distance through Double Bay, down to Rose Bay, and across to Bondi.

Arabella was waiting for them at the finish line, handing out towels and cold water. Mack and Daisy were both sweaty and exhausted by then, but nothing could dampen their euphoria, especially when Arabella checked their fundraising tally and they found out they had raised $22,000 for the Children's Medical Research Institute. Mack lifted both hands into the air in a triumphant salute and turned around to find Daisy, who was shaking hands with one of the event organisers.

Without warning, he picked her up and spun her around, before setting her back down and taking her face into his hands. He looked down at her, his eyes searching hers for what felt like the longest moment ever, before he dipped her backwards and crushed her lips to his, kissing her hot and hard in front of the cheering crowd. This time she kissed him back with equal intensity and was rewarded by the feel of his heart beating overtime, knowing full well it had nothing to do with the race they had just run. Arabella rolled her eyes and looked away as their kiss continued until the news crew arrived and she had to separate them for a brief interview.

Mack and Daisy stopped kissing and opened their eyes, blinking at one another hotly as Arabella introduced them to the journalist who was there to do a piece about the funds they had raised.

Still holding on to each other's hands, Mack explained to the camera that his little sister had been diagnosed with cancer when she was eleven years old and that, sadly, she hadn't lived to see her twelfth birthday.

"But today kids like Tess can beat their cancer, and that is because of the awesome work of CMRI. I am so happy to be fundraising for them and I wanted to say thank you to everyone who donated to me and Daisy today. Your support will literally mean the whole world for a family going through what mine did 15 years ago. Thank you!" Mack lifted Daisy's hand up in yet another triumphant salute before kissing her again, much to the crowd's delight.

The last of Daisy's defences melted away as she listened to him tell the story of Tess. She realised she had gotten this funny, kind guy all wrong. Looking up at him adoringly, she finally admitted to herself what she had long suspected —she had fallen for Mack. Hook, line and sinker.

After the interview, everyone was milling around for a while, asking for Mack's autograph. Mack's phone rang and he let go of her hand to answer it, moving away so he could hear the caller more clearly. Daisy couldn't hear what he said, but he was smiling when he hung up and turned back to her.

"Hey, that was my friend Shaun. We are going to catch

up this afternoon before we go to the Ivy. Do you mind? It's his big night and he must be nervous." Daisy and Mack were going to the launch of Shaun's new album at the Ivy nightclub in the city later that night.

"That's fine. I can see you there. I have the invite! Have fun!" Daisy waved Mack off, but he turned back and looked down at Daisy earnestly.

"You really have changed my life, Daisy Gardiner. See, I've even taken to remembering your name!" he said, kissing her lightly on her forehead before disappearing into the crowd to find his ride home.

————

Daisy was giddy with excitement as she dressed for this penultimate public date. After her afternoon revelation, she couldn't wait to see Mack again. And she was going to get to meet one of his friends as well. She felt like he was finally letting her into his life.

Arabella sat on the bed frowning, watching Daisy with increasing worry.

"Hey, I know Mack has been really nice over the last two weeks, but please don't forget he is still Mack Boddington, the arrogant prick who made you accidentally rain on the whole Fashion festival parade," she said, nervously chewing her nails as she waited for Daisy's reaction.

"Oh Arabella, I know. He is a dick. But he is a very sweet guy underneath all the arrogance and bravado. Ok, how do I look?" Daisy turned and twirled for Arabella, showing off her green mini dress, with long flared sleeves. The material was from India, ornately embroidered chiffon encrusted with small green glass beads and sequins.

"You look amazing Daisy…I am sure Dan would think so too. Remember him?"

Arabella looked at her friend, filled with guilt at having pushed her into this crazy escapade with Mack. If this jeopardised Daisy's chance at a real romance with Dan, she would never forgive herself.

Daisy was also filled with guilt, thinking back to the last time she had seen Dan. She still couldn't tell Arabella that she had snuck out to see him. And that she didn't feel the same way she felt about him. Arabella had been right about Dan all along. It was hard keeping secrets from her friend, but she knew this was just how it had to be for now.

"I can't think about Dan right now. I need to see if this is real."

"Daisy, I don't think it is. You have to be prepared for that."

"Just let me figure this out, AB," Daisy snapped as she walked out, upset that Arabella seemed so insistent on bursting her Mack bubble.

———

Daisy's bad mood had fully evaporated by the time she reached the Ivy, and she was eagerly counting down the seconds until she could see Mack again. The security detail quickly ushered her past the queue and into the foyer, where she was escorted into a private elevator that took her up to the top floor, to nightclub's infamous pool bar. Tonight it was invitation only as Shaun, otherwise known as DJ Dasaani, launched his new album of electronic dance beats.

Mack was dancing next to Shaun at the mixing desk, and he looked up as Daisy walked in. He leant over and said something to Shaun, who tilted his head to one side and nodded appreciatively. Mack outlined the shape of a woman's curves with his hands and although she wasn't known for her lip-reading skills, Daisy swore he said 'get me some' as he was making the lewd gestures. Despite his appreciation for her form, he didn't come down from the DJ booth, so Daisy turned and walked over to the bar.

Eventually Shaun took a break from spinning his records and he and Mack joined Daisy at the bar.

"Gardenia! Let me introduce you to my very best friend in the world. Shaun Dyson. Dasaani, meet the girl I am faux-beauxing, as my canny publicist keeps saying!

"Hi there, girl, you are a pretty one, aren't you?" Shaun was obviously high as a kite. Mack laughed loudly at Shaun's attempt to be smooth.

So was Mack, Daisy realised.

"Are you ok?" she asked in concern, pulling Mack gently to the side so that they could talk for a moment. But he pulled away and moved back to Shaun, who had returned with another round of drinks.

"I'm fine little Daisy...here have another drink while we go back up an' spin some more tunes..."

Daisy stayed at the bar as Mack and Shaun, giggling like schoolboys, returned to the decks. She sipped her second drink slowly, already feeling a little tipsy from her first martini, and watched as Mack stood next to his friend, bopping out of time to the music.

After a few minutes, Daisy relaxed as she watched Mack shimmy and shake on the stage.

She smiled. He looked so good up there and she just wanted him to come back down so she could run her hands over that famously toned belly of his and then further down to...

Woah Daisy, that's a bit full on for you, she thought to herself sternly. *This is a public place!*

Yes Daisy, she also said to herself, *this is a public place. You can't touch your ridiculously hot boyfriend here at the bar, or anywhere really, because he is not really your boyfriend!*

Bugger off Daisy, her next thought instructed. *What's the point of dating a ridiculously hot celebrity if I can't touch him wherever and whenever I want! Plus, he did kiss me several times.* Her thoughts continued triumphantly.

Suddenly Mack was next to her, dripping with sweat from his excited dance routine.

"What do you think Gardeen, his album is ace, isn't it?"

Daisy blinked and looked around her. Shaun and Mack were down from the platform and standing next to her, Mack looking at her intently while Shaun was shaking hands and signing autographs.

"Is it over?" she asked in confusion. "But didn't I just get here?"

Beside her, Shaun laughed theatrically. "Glad to see your babe was so into my music, Boddington!" he said, punching Mack on the shoulder.

"Babe, you've been standing there watching for an hour. Come on, let's go out into the private booth."

Mack took hold of Daisy's arm and started walking

towards the side of the pool, where several VIP only booths were located. Although private, the booths were still on full display to the rest of the party, who were continuing to dance on the platform across the water.

"Even the VIP room has a VIP room," Daisy murmured to herself with a giggle, before watching a trail of phosphorescence snake down her arm where Mack was touching her.

Mack was striding slightly ahead of her, so Daisy had an uninterrupted view of his broad shoulders, which were flexing slightly as he walked. She just wanted to reach out and run her hands down his back and under his shirt, to the hard, smooth muscles she knew were there. She still hadn't touched his six-pack yet and suddenly it was all she could think about.

By the time they reached their booth, Daisy was vibrating with desire, and she sat down on Mack's lap and kissed him hard, sliding her hands up and down his chest feverishly. She was too distracted to notice the cheers and whoops from the other party guests who had clocked the sexy celebrity shenanigans.

"You are so damn hot, Mack. How can you be so hot? You feel so good. Let's go back to your hotel because I want to take your clothes off and see if you look as good as you feel."

Mack looked around at the party.

"Yeah, this is boring, come on sweetheart, let's go..." he said, scooping Daisy up over his shoulder and carrying her out of the bar, while she laughed hilariously, completely unaware her knickers where flashing to the entire nightclub and a few thrilled paparazzi.

Luckily, Mack was staying just up the road at the Four Seasons. Daisy's vision was getting fuzzier and fuzzier and all she could think of was getting Mack into his room and into bed, as he piggybacked her down George Street and into the night.

Bloody hell! giggled Daisy to herself. *This is really happening...I'm about to make out with a movie star!*

THIRTEEN

SydneyShhh! *Bondi babe Daisy Gardiner 'macking' on hottie Boddington! Click here for all the sordid photos of their Ivy sexathon!*

———

The next thing Daisy remembered was a dry, scratchy throat and hot burning eyes.

She opened one eye experimentally. She was in a hotel room. She wriggled. She was definitely in a bed. She turned her head slightly and saw Mack, completely naked, spread-eagled on the floor next to her, sound asleep.

Sweet baby Jane, she groaned inwardly. Even snoring his head off, passed out on the floor, Mack Boddington was still the sexiest man she had ever seen...in real life or on film. She smiled for a second before flashes of memory starting creeping their way back in to her mind.

She looked down and realised she was also completely naked. Suddenly she was overcome with the most urgent need to throw up and with a small yelp, she grabbed the sheet and made a dash for the bathroom.

After a few minutes, she could hear Mack knocking on the door.

"Are you quite done in there?" he queried, in that arrogant, bored voice she recognised from the Fashion Festival launch party.

"What is going on?" asked Daisy, emerging from the bathroom, her face ashen and her hands still shaking.

"Oh man, I hate it when groupies puke in my bathroom" Mack said disdainfully, not looking at her as he went into the bathroom and slammed the door.

Daisy could hear her phone beeping like crazy, but she couldn't see it. She needed to find it, to find out what time it was. But she also needed to find out what was wrong with Mack. He seemed like a completely different person today.

"Mack, did we sleep together last night?" she called, locating her phone as she drew the curtain to let more light into the stuffy hotel room. Below her the Opera House and the Sydney Harbour Bridge sparkled in the mid-morning sunlight.

What the hell? She thought, desperately trying to recall how they ended up in a posh Circular Quay hotel. Her phone was still beeping.

Where are you? What is going on? What happened last night?

Daisy looked from the harbour vista to Arabella's texts in confusion, still not sure where she was exactly, and clicked on the link Arabella had sent.

Suddenly Daisy had the urge to vomit again. There she was, on full display for the world to see, grinding on Mack's lap, her eyes rolling backwards and her hand down his pants. She looked terrible - like she was drugged and out of control.

Whoa Mack Daddy! Is the shine starting to rub off Bondi's golden girl? Click here for exclusive photos and a NSFW video of Daisy's sleazy night out at the Ivy with Mack!

Suddenly memories of the night came flooding back, as shame burnt crimson across her cheeks.

"What the hell Mack! Did you put something in my drink? Did you drug me?"

Daisy looked down at the sheet she was currently wearing as a toga.

"Eww! Did you have sex with me while I was passed out?" Daisy shivered incredulously and fought the urge to be sick again as the reality of the situation dawned on her.

Across the room, Mack emerged from the bathroom, looking like a new man.

He paused when he saw Daisy, still standing in the middle of the room wrapped in the sheet, and winced slightly. For a moment it seemed like he was going to say something. But Mack's expression became unreadable again as he stood in the doorway, smoothing out the cuffs of his blazer.

"You were begging me for it!" he sneered, laughing at her discomfort.

"Why would you do this? I'm helping you out! How could you be so mean? And so gross to take advantage of a drunk girl! And I thought you liked me. You told me you wouldn't hurt me."

"What did you think Daisy? I'm an actor! It's my job to

fool people into believing me when I'm playing a character. And trust me...this thing we've been doing, this is all just an act. I've been playing the happy, wholesome guy, with the cute girlfriend and sad childhood story. You are going to be free to go back to your old life after tonight. Back to Dan. It's all just an act Gardenia, don't you remember?"

"Stop fucking calling me that!" shouted Daisy, clutching the sheet tighter around her and collecting her clothes from around the room. "Oh my goodness...did you really even have a sister who died? You made that all up, didn't you! Mack, you are so stupid, people can google this shit now, you'll be caught out." Daisy went into the bathroom and quickly changed back into her beautiful green dress.

"Mack, seriously, what's going on?" she continued, now fully dressed. She looked Mack directly in the eye for a moment, before hurriedly picking up the contents of her small purse, from where it had been strewn the previous night. "What happened?"

"Go home Daisy."

"Mack, I don't understand..."

"I said, go home Daisy."

Daisy closed her eyes and took a deep breath. "Go to hell Mack."

Mack turned his back to Daisy and didn't say anything, so she walked out, slamming the door hard behind her.

She held it together until she got home, but as soon as she walked into the lounge room and saw Royce and Arabella, she sat on the floor and cried.

"I really liked him, and he is such a jerk."

Royce and Arabella came and sat next to her on the

floor, both of them putting their arms around her and cocooning her in between them, the same way they did after her accident.

As soon as she stopped crying, Daisy recounted the sordid night's events.

"Man, I want to punch his smug little face," said Arabella violently.

"There are quite a few people I want to punch in the face today," said Royce, his usually gentle voice angry.

"What do you mean?" asked Daisy, looking between her brother and Arabella.

"Daisy, we have something else to tell you that is not going to make you feel great. Dan did an interview with a national newspaper, and they ran it today. He talks about your love affair and how you abandoned him to chase after a celebrity. He talks about your accident and how he didn't think someone like Mack would be into you because of your scars."

"What the hell?" exclaimed Daisy in disbelief. "Show me!"

Royce sheepishly produced his iPad from under the lounge cushion and opened up a news app.

"That's where you were planning to hide this from me?" she asked with a laugh, loving how impractical, but always so considerate, her big brother was.

Her laughter stopped, however, when she saw the article. Inside there was a series of photos of Daisy that Dan had taken at his place, photos that showed some of her scars. She hadn't realised they were visible when Dan had been taking the photos in his back garden just a few weeks ago. But here they were, on full display for the whole world to see. Worst of all, Dan had claimed they had been in love but that she had cruelly dumped him for a chance to be with a celebrity. It made her seem shallow and hungry for fame. Combined with the photos from last night, she doubted if anyone would ever believe she was actually a nice person, ever again.

"Oh!" she gasped, putting her hand over her mouth as she read, unable to say anything. This was coming close to being the worst day of her life. Surely the sale would be off by now. Daisy thought about her proposal to Glass. There was no way they would be interested in her proposal after all this had hit the press. This was not the good type of publicity a prospective buyer wanted for a brand.

"Right," said Arabella after a few minutes of silence had passed. She heaved herself up off the floor. For someone who was barely showing, she felt a million times heavier than normal. Looking down at her husband, she wondered if it was emotional baggage and not baby baggage that she was carrying.

"What do you want to do, Daisy?"

Daisy looked down at the article. "I want this to go away," she said bitterly. "I want this, and the photos from last night, to all go away. And I want a retraction and an apology for publishing them in the first place. And I want to kick Dan's teeth in." And I want last night to have all been a bad dream, she added silently.

"Ok then, time to get this train back on the tracks!"

First, she dialled Mack. "Mack Boddington, you are not that smart and you are not particularly talented. All you have going for you right now is that you are devastatingly handsome, and you have me as a publicist. So if you want to ever, and I mean EVER work again, anywhere in the world, you need to get your drug addled balls down here to Bondi, with a white suit for the party tonight and be ready to be so fucking apologetic, because me and my very tall husband are both gagging to be beat the crap out of you, you got it? Be here in an hour," she shouted into her phone, before hanging up on him.

"I'm sorry Daisy," she said after she had caught her breath. "But that man cannot be trusted to stay sober and presentable. This will all be over very soon, I promise."

"AB, you can't be serious," Royce raged. "Why are you keeping up the pretence? This guy hurt my sister, your best friend? Why are you bothering to have anything more to do with him? Surely enough is enough?"

Arabella looked at her husband coldly. "Because this is my job, and I am good at it, and I know how to fix this. I'm sorry you have no faith in me, but I'm not stopping just because you think I should."

Next Arabella called a friend at the paper which had published Dan's story and had the rights to the photos.

"Listen honey, if you squash this for me, I will owe you big time. And by big time, I mean tickets to the White Party tonight, as well as front row seats at the next two big concerts of your choice..." Arabella was quiet for a moment. "Uh huh," she said.

"Yep, I understand," she replied.

After a few more seconds, Arabella threw in her last-minute poker chip. "I can give you an exclusive interview with Nan Sinclair."

Nan Sinclair, despite being one of the world's top models and having been seen out and about for the last two weeks, was notoriously shy about giving media interviews. But Arabella knew her well and knew she could count on her for this huge favour.

"Great! Deal. Thanks Hilda! We'll courier the tickets over right away."

Arabella then called the pap who owned the photos from the Ivy and coolly offered him five thousand dollars for the images. Royce looked at her, both relieved that Daisy's problems were being sorted out and aghast that she was spending so much money when they were saving for the baby.

Arabella hung up, glaring back at her husband, who was now red-faced with anger. "Someone already bought them. Stop looking at me like that, Royce," she retorted.

"Arabella, I want to help Daisy just as much as you, but you can't just offer that much money without talking to me first."

"That money was mine from the consulting job I did before I started the company. Daisy would've paid me back whenever she was ready," Arabella snapped back.

Daisy looked at Arabella and Royce, now sitting at opposite ends of the dining table, glaring at each other. Arabella was furious and Royce looked exhausted, having arrived on an overnight flight from Bangkok that morning. Was everything broken today?

"But who would want to buy those photos? What can they do with them?" asked Daisy, trying to distract Arabella and Royce from yet another argument.

Arabella turned her attention back to Daisy.

"It is hard to say right now. It could be someone with a grudge against Mack. He puts people offside easily. We are just going to have to wait and see what happens next. We will sort it out though, Daisy. I promise you that."

Arabella sighed wearily.

"Why don't we all have a few moments of quiet before Mack arrives? I don't know about you, Daisy, but I could really use a nap right about now."

Leaving Royce in the lounge room, the two girls lay down on Daisy's bed, like they did when they were kids and were soon fast asleep.

———

Fifty-five minutes later, there was a small knock at the door. It was Mack. As he walked inside the apartment, he saw Royce and took a step back.

"Luckily for you, you idiot, you are not the only dick-head we are dealing right now. Get inside and sit down and shut the hell up," Royce barked at him. Mack walked inside and meekly sat down, not looking at Daisy, not even when she walked up and kicked him in the shin.

By 5pm, the four of them were standing at the door, dressed head to toe in white. Arabella was issuing instructions with the ease of a drill sergeant.

"Ok, this is about to happen. Mack, this is not only the closing party of the Sydney Fashion Festival, but it is also your farewell party. Assuming your stupid antics last night haven't jeopardised your movie deals, you are packed and flying to LA on Tuesday morning. So, if you want that to happen, you need to be on your best behaviour."

"Oh, and Mack, one last thing." Arabella walked up to Mack and kicked him hard on the same shin that Daisy had kicked a few hours earlier. "If you ever drug my best friend, or any woman for that matter, ever again, that won't be the body part I kick. Got it?" Mack nodded, still not speaking to anyone.

Daisy's phone rang, and they all looked at it. No one was game enough to answer it.

It was Lola.

Daisy looked at Arabella and Royce, who both looked back at her nervously.

"Someone is going to have to answer it," she said.

Finally, Royce grabbed the phone and put Lola on speaker phone.

"Hey Mum. It's Royce. You're on speaker and the girls are here."

"Royce Gardiner, what the hell are you three playing at down there? Daisy, what on earth are you doing? Bill and Jeff and I are really worried about you guys, and we are really angry that you are all behaving so terribly. This is not how we raised you! And this Mack fellow. Arabella, I know he is your client, but honey, what are you doing? I think you three better make some plans to come home, don't you? Clearly your chakras are way out of alignment right now or something is off, and what you need is some reiki and a good talking to! All three of you, and Mack too."

"Mum, we are late for an event," Royce replied vaguely. "We'll call you tomorrow and tell you everything, I promise."

Daisy looked around at each of the three people standing in front of her. It was only then that she realised Royce and Arabella hadn't looked at each other or spoken directly to one another since their earlier altercation. She also realised that all four of them looked ghastly and were in need of two days' worth of sleep. Lola was right. They had all been behaving so badly and while she doubted it was their chakras, something was clearly out of balance in all their lives.

She looked at her brother, so tall and handsome in his white cargo pants and short-sleeved, button-up shirt. His face was frozen in fury at the events of the day and the antics of both Dan and Mack. She also rightly guessed that he was still angry at Arabella for putting her in this position. Despite her exhaustion and misery, she tried not to laugh as he glowered menacingly at Mack.

Arabella was immaculate as always, but Daisy knew her well enough to know she was struggling not to cry. Tonight, she was wearing a long, silk dress with a wrap-around neckline and a white sash sitting just under the bust. It was quite Grecian and a little like Daisy's toga from the hotel room this morning. Daisy stifled a hysterical giggle as Arabella resumed her stern instructions, seemingly oblivious to Lola's scolding.

Daisy looked over at Mack, who was sulking against the doorframe, sullen and hurting from the drugs and in desperate need of something to take the edge off. He was wearing a white blazer with a tight white t-shirt and white jeans. It made his blue eyes appear even brighter. From a distance Daisy knew he would still look like the super-charged, sexy celebrity he was. It was only up close you could tell how much pain he was in.

Daisy looked down miserably at her own dress. She had been planning to wear a new creation but the events of the last twenty-four hours had left her in dire need of rest and so she had spent most of the afternoon napping. Instead, she was wearing the same dress she worn to the Lost at Sea premiere party. It was the party where she had first met Mack, she remembered with a jolt. She looked at him again, her eyes big and sad as she thought back to how uncomplicated her life had been just a few weeks ago.

Maybe me and Dan would have had a chance, she thought with a sad sigh, before correcting herself. *No, I can't ever think that. He gave a story about me to the national press to get back at me. That is not the action of a good guy.* Lost in her own reverie, she didn't see the anguished look in Mack's eyes as he took in her miserable expression.

We all look so glamourous, Daisy thought sadly. *So glamourous and so bloody miserable. It really just goes to show that life in the bubble of celebrity is definitely not all it's cracked up to be. You really can never tell what is really going on behind the scenes.*

FOURTEEN

Oh-Em-G *It's the question on EVERYONE'S lips tonight... will Mack and Daisy be at the White Party or was last night's Ivy escapade the last we will see of this adorable couple? Oh-Em-G hopes we haven't seen the last of 'Maisy'!*

———

The White Party was perhaps the second most glamorous and extravagant event of Sydney's Fashion Festival. It was the swimwear showcase, and it was always held at Bondi Beach's Icebergs, the dramatic ocean pool creating the most spectacular backdrop for a sunset fashion parade. Guests were asked to wear white to blend in with the chalky cliffs, so that the blue water of the pool and the vibrant blaze of swimwear remained the focus of the show.

Arabella led the group down the small pathway beside the apartment building, to the gate that discreetly sat a few metres past the entrance to Icebergs. Perched on one side of the entrance, in a roped area, over 50 national and international photographers were jostling each to get as close to the front as possible. Famous faces were already arriving, and the cameras were flashing.

"Listen," Arabella said, casting an experienced eye over the set up. "If we slip through the gate and around the left side of the photographers, we'll be on the carpet before they know we are there. From there it will only be a minute or so in front of the cameras before we get down the stairs to the pool."

Arabella's plan seemed to work, and they reached the top of the ramp unnoticed. Daisy watched as Arabella and Royce went ahead. Royce instinctively put his arm around Arabella as the paparazzi recognised their colleague and started snapping, but Arabella stiffened and pulled away. *AB doesn't enjoy being the story Royce, you know that;* she thought to herself sadly, as Royce dropped his arm and stalked off ahead, clearly feeling unwanted.

"Arabella, where's Mack and Daisy tonight? Oh, Daisy! Over here! How do feel about Dan's article in the Tele today? Are you and Mack still on?"

Startled by all the flashes and shouting, Daisy let out a small cry of alarm. Mack reached out to grab Daisy's hand, to let her know he was there, but she dropped her head and pulled away, pushing forward to join Arabella, who put her arm around Daisy and quickly escorted her down the ramp towards the private entrance into the pool.

"Mack, mate, is it true? How do you feel about Daisy's expose in the papers today? Are you two still dating after that?"

Mack turned his back to the cameras and followed

Daisy and Arabella, his only response a raised middle finger to the assembled media.

The crowd went wild, and the cameras went into overdrive as the paparazzi snapped Australia's hottest young star gesturing at them obscenely. It was guaranteed to run on the front page of all the major papers the next day.

Once inside, the chaos of the media scrum melted away, as the outside world gave way to the tranquil pool, sparkling in the late afternoon sun. This year, a long strip of reinforced Perspex ran vertically down the pool, which Daisy imagined would make it seem like the models were walking on water. Daisy looked at the runway anxiously as she walked down the stairs to the pool deck. *Bloody hell, no one bigger than a child could walk across that without breaking it,* she thought, shaking her head at the absurdity of it all.

Glass had several pieces in the showcase this evening and Ben and Stu were already sitting in the front row. They waved them over and introduced them to Sasha, their sixteen-year-old daughter.

"Wow, our parents never took us anywhere this cool when we were sixteen," laughed Arabella. "I hope this gets you heaps of fame at school!"

"It's ok, I guess," replied Sasha, looking around nervously. "I'm actually doing work experience at Underwater World back home this week. I think I would prefer to be there, even though the fish smell so bad."

Daisy sat down next to Sasha, biting her thumbnail as she nervously wondered why Ben and Stu hadn't said anything about her email.

"Thank you for your proposal, Daisy," Ben said, leaning across Arabella and Sasha to squeeze her hand. "You had some excellent suggestions, and we are always so excited to hear from other creatives. But I think..."

Ben was cut off by the sound of drums being pounded to signal the start of the show.

Daisy felt like she was going to throw up. She was sure Ben had just been about to say no to her proposal. A rejection on top of everything else today was more than she could handle.

"What proposal?" hissed Arabella down the row. "What is going on?"

"I'll tell you later," Daisy whispered back, trying to hold back tears of humiliation. The last thing she wanted to do was explain how Ben and Stu had rejected her in front of them.

They settled in to watch the show, and soon all thoughts of the awful last twenty-four hours were forgotten. The crowd gasped as the tiki torches lining the edges of the pool were lit up just as the sun dipped over the horizon. Suddenly the jangly sounds of California surf guitars filled up the air and spotlights revealed the surprise guests. The Beach Boys were standing high above them on the deck where Arabella and Daisy went to yoga, the strains of their famous song, *Wouldn't It Be Nice*, filling the air as one by one the models appeared, sauntering casually down the stairs and across the clear walkway. Clearly the swimwear trend for next summer was harking back to the late eighties and early nineties again, with lots of geometric prints and vibrant, fluro colours. The show was dazzling and a lot of fun, with the crowd singing along to all the songs. As the Beach Boys launched into *God Only Knows*, Daisy looked across to see Mack looking at her, his expression both sneering and tormented. Daisy quickly looked away. She was feeling sick and exhausted and couldn't deal with his eccentricities right now.

Towards the end of the show, Arabella looked around and realised that Mack had disappeared.

"Bloody hell," she hissed to Royce and Daisy. "Mack has gone. Did you see him go?" They looked around frantically, but by now the sun had set and it was hard to tell who was who amidst all the white clad guests.

Once the show was over and the rapturous applause had ended, Arabella sent them off into the crowd to find Mack. It was quite a party, and it seemed like everyone Daisy had met since she had arrived in Sydney was there. Wait staff dressed in white shorts and sandshoes, topped with fluro green t-shirts, wove through the famous crowd, handing out blue and pink and orange cocktails. Lozza Rothermere-Smythe was holding court at one end of the pool. Sylvia and the others from the Glass shoot were sitting several rows above them, chatting to Saffron from Thread Bare.

Even the Hollywood elite had stayed in town to attend the closing party and as Daisy walked tiredly though the crowd looking for Mack, she vaguely noticed Margot and Rose chatting excitedly to Lara and Sam, while Cate and Hugh taste-tested their 80s-coloured drinks a few steps above. Down on the pool level, the country's most respected news breakfast host was doing his best to seduce Alba Andrews, but Alba was more interested in the swimsuit models who had started to trickle out into the party, dressed in white kaftans with multi coloured fluorescent bangles stacked up each forearm. Daisy looked around and felt nothing but pity for these people.

Is this all really worth it? She thought sadly, before she continued her search for Mack in the crowd.

At the other end of the pool, Arabella and Brian had found the studio executives who were there to formally announce Mack's contract and his departure to start shooting the new Michael Bay action film.

"So, where is the man of the hour?" asked one of the suited entertainment lawyers. "We have the contract for signing, so as soon as we get him down here, this thing is a done deal!"

Arabella exchanged a brief worried look with Brian before turning back to the lawyers.

"How wonderful," she said with a tight smile. "Let me go find him and we will get the ink on the paper!"

Arabella and Brian quickly caught up with Daisy and Royce at the bottom of the stairs.

"I am going to kill that man!" muttered Arabella, still smiling and waving to people she knew in the crowd. "I want this over and done with so we can go back to our regular lives and forget any of us ever met Mack Boddington."

Suddenly Daisy heard Mack's unmistakable drawl up on the third step of the terrace and her heart sank. He was clearly high and had his hands around the waist of one of the young waitresses, in full view of the party and the studio executives. Shaun, his awful DJ friend from the night before, was standing next to him, along with a bevy of young soapie stars, all hanging on to every word he was saying.

"As if I would ever seriously hook up with someone like that," he was laughing, nuzzling the waitress and sliding his hand under her shirt as he talked. "I think that Dan guy was right. She is completely messed up. She got so high last night at Shaun's party, and she threw herself at me, I don't know why, she knew all along I was just her faux beau, I guess it was the only way she could get up the courage to make a move on me." Mack looked down from his perch and for a moment their eyes met, his cold and angry and hers, wide and hurt, filling with tears.

"Oh my goodness, why is he doing this?" gasped Daisy, looking across Arabella and Royce. Without waiting for them to answer, she turned and fled up the stairs and out into the darkness of night, desperate to escape the clicking and flashing of the assembled paparazzi.

———

Seeking solace, Daisy ran to the one thing that always comforted her. The ocean. She didn't stop until she reached the water's edge and felt the cool salt water engulf her bare feet. High above, the White Party continued to celebrate the last gasp of summer, with sugary pop songs wafting out over the dark ocean and a rainbow of lights shimmering up into the dark sky. The ocean however, had turned dark and menacing, which matched Daisy's mood very well, and she could see flickers of lightening on the horizon.

How could I have been so stupid? Humiliated and betrayed by two guys in 24 hours? I have got rotten taste in men, she thought bitterly.

"Daisy, wait up!" She turned at the sound of her name

and peered through the darkness, suddenly realising how vulnerable she was, in the darkness of the south end of the beach.

She wiped away her tears and turned to face the voice. It was Dan.

"Oh Dan," she cried in relief, momentarily forgetting how much she hated him. "Oh it's you! Thank goodness!"

"Oh Daisy, I am so glad you aren't mad!" he exclaimed happily, reaching out to take her hand. "I have been sitting down here, knowing you were up there at the party, wishing like crazy I could go up and tell you how sorry I am for hurting you. I am so glad you came down. It's like you knew I was here, waiting for you..."

"Wait, no, that's not what I meant," cried Daisy in alarm, snatching back her hand. "I meant, I am glad you are not a crazy psycho." She looked up at him, realisation dawning across her angry face. "Actually Dan, you are, you know that? You are a crazy psycho. That's all I can see when I look at you."

She glared at Dan, his curly hair and crinkly eyes no longer making her stomach flip-flop. Now the sight of him was making her stomach churn and coil, as she recalled the horrible things he had said in the newspaper article and the anger she had been feeling all day began to erupt.

"What the hell man, I can't believe you could betray me like that," she shouted angrily, wiping more tears from her eyes. "I thought you were a good guy, but you are awful! Why would you do that me?"

Dan squeezed his eyes shut for a second and sighed. "I'm so sorry Daisy. I am so sorry. But you were going to leave me for Mack, anyway. When I saw you guys on the beach, at that photo shoot, I knew I had lost you. And that paparazzi guy was right there. And I really needed the money."

"Wait, you got paid for that?" cried Daisy in disbelief, taking a step back. "You seriously, literally, sold me out?" She turned, fighting the urge to be sick, before the next betrayal hit home.

"But I've seen you since then," she gasped in disbelief. "I came over to your house and you kissed me, and you had already sold the story."

"Daisy, I'm sorry. I wanted you so bad. Please let me make it up to you..."

Dan reached out to put his arms around Daisy, but she quickly pulled away and put some distance between them. She turned back to face Dan, his face just visible on the gloomy beach.

"Why would you ever think that I would want to be with you after doing something like that?" she shouted angrily.

She waited, but he didn't have anything to say. He just hung his head in embarrassment instead.

"I can never, ever forgive you for what you've done to me," she continued, taking a deep breath. "You know that, right? I never want to see you again."

With that, Daisy turned and left him standing on the sand as she finally made her way home to bed. If she was lucky, she would wake up tomorrow and this would all have been a very bad dream.

———

Back at the party, the studio executives had cornered Arabella and Brian and were shouting at them for not being able to keep their client under control. One of them pulled out a sheath of papers and ripped it up dramatically before stalking off up the stairs.

"Well, that's the Michael Bay contract gone," sighed Brian sadly, looking up at Mack who was still holding court up on the terrace.

Next in line was Saffron, from Thread Bare.

"Arabella, this is a disgrace. The deal with Daisy Gardiner is off. I am utterly appalled—after everything we have done. We absolutely cannot be associated with such drama!"

Arabella and Brian watched speechlessly as Saffron and her entourage stalked off.

Mack looked down and saw Arabella and Brian huddled together and sauntered down the terrace steps to join them, oblivious to the multiple crises they were currently managing.

"Agent! PR Queen! PR Queen's Husband! How is everything down here? When are we making the big speech? La-La Land here I come!" he said cheerily, as he joined them by the pool.

"Oh my God Mack! You are the dumbest, most ridiculous idiot ever!" growled Brian, slapping his own forehead in exasperation.

Mack looked around at them, taking in their angry faces. "Wait, is this about Daisy? Where is she, anyway? Shouldn't she be here for the big announcement?"

Arabella looked at Mack in frustration. "The Bay contract is done, Mack. They just clocked your little performance up on the steps, all the terrible things you said about Daisy. You are obviously completely high...where did you get the drugs from, anyway?"

"Arabella, it's a fashion party. Who doesn't have drugs here?"

Arabella shook her head, anger finally boiling over. "You know what Mack, I quit. I refuse to do business with you anymore."

She turned to walk away, but changed her mind and turned back. "And you know what else, you stupid, arrogant dickhead?" Without waiting for an answer, she punched Mack squarely on the nose. "That is for hurting my best friend!"

Startled, Mack fell back into the pool, where he floated, spluttering and splashing, to the cheers of Royce and Brian. Stu and Ben broke into spontaneous applause, while Sasha looked on with wide eyes. Crazy things always happened when she accompanied her parents to their work parties.

"You guys are a funny family!" laughed Stu.

"But Mack certainly had that coming," added Ben thoughtfully.

Arabella stood on the side of the pool, rubbing her knuckles gingerly, glaring down at the bedraggled heartthrob bobbing in the turquoise water. She turned to Royce and held out her hands.

"I'm so sorry babe, I've been really crap, getting caught up in this mess. I promise from here on there will be no more jerks, ok, only quality clients!"

Arabella took a deep breath and looked up at her handsome and lovely husband. He was her best friend, and she was so tired of fighting with him.

"Royce, I am so scared about this baby!" She blurted out, relieved to finally admit the truth to him. "I'm scared of what this will mean for my business, and I am scared about how it will hurt and how it will change our lives. I love you so much and I want us to start a family. I just didn't think it would be this soon, and I wasn't ready for it."

Royce stepped forward and hugged his wife tightly. "I love you Arabella. I'm scared too! But you are the most amazing woman I've ever known, and you will rock the crap out of being a mum, the way you do everything in your life. Your career is so important and I'm so sorry I haven't been more supportive. We will find a way to make it work when the baby comes, I promise."

Mack was still floating in the pool below them. "What do you mean, baby? Are you having a baby? Why didn't you tell me? That's awesome!"

Royce sighed and shook his head. Leaning over, he reached down and fished out the wayward tv star.

"I've really fucked up, haven't I?" asked Mack mournfully, as he climbed out of the pool. He appeared to have sobered up a little from the shock of the cold water.

"You really have," Arabella said severely. "You'll be lucky if you can salvage any contract at all after this performance."

"No, I don't care about that, I mean with Daisy." Mack looked up Arabella and Royce from where he was sprawled on the edge of the pool, dripping wet and bedraggled, his handsome blue eyes full of sorrow and regret. "I thought getting rid of the photos would be enough, but I don't think she even noticed."

"What do you mean?" asked Arabella cautiously, still glaring down at Mack.

"We'd better dry him off and get him out of here," said Royce, noticing the clicking and flashing from the select paparazzi who had been lucky enough to get invited into the after party. "I think he has some explaining to do."

"You know, I've always liked that young man," said Stu with a grin, as they watched Royce and Arabella escort Mack up the stairs.

"Your head is always turned by a handsome man," replied his husband drily.

"My head is only ever turned by one handsome man, and he is standing right next to me," laughed Stu, kissing Ben tenderly and reaching down to squeeze his hand.

"Eww, gross!" said Sasha, rolling her eyes dramatically. "Parents are so embarrassing!"

Fifteen

Dramorama *Holy smokes Batman, DID-THAT-JUST-HAPPEN? The White Party is renowned for its spice and scandal, but this year it has delivered in spades! Honourable mention to PR Queen Arabella McCarthy punching her client Mack Boddington in the face and into the pool, but that is nothing compared to Izzy, Kingston and Brandon's debut as TV's newest throuple...or the accidental outing of Jax Turpin and Mike Sokoloff's secret love affair! The Dramorama kids can't catch our breath #BEST-NIGHTEVER!*

———

The next morning, Daisy woke with a heavy heart. She lay in bed for a few minutes, letting the events of the previous two nights swirl around in her mind. Mack's betrayal after the Ivy party, his humiliating display at Icebergs, Dan's article and his pathetic grovelling on the beach last night, Ben's response to her proposal. It was all so awful.

But time to get up and face whatever fresh horror awaits me today, she thought bitterly.

Out on the balcony, Royce and Arabella were having breakfast. Daisy immediately noticed that their permafrost had melted, and things seemed to be much better between them. That was something, at least. Although the day was grey and cool, Daisy slipped on her sunglasses and joined them at the table.

"Well, you two look chipper this morning," said Daisy sourly as she poured herself a coffee.

"Good morning to you too, sunshine," said Royce merrily, exchanging an amused glance with his wife.

"You missed one hell of party last night," said Arabella, buttering some toast and passing it over to the moping Daisy. "It's a shame you slept through it!"

"I wish I could have slept through it all," replied Daisy. "Actually, I went to the beach and ran into Dan. He had the nerve to think that we would get back together. After all he did," she continued with a shudder. "After that, I came home and went to bed."

"We checked in on you when we got back and you were fast asleep. We didn't want to wake you," said Royce.

"Yeah, I really needed that sleep," yawned Daisy. "So, the rest of the party was pretty wild, hey? How did it end up?"

Arabella looked at Daisy carefully. "After Mack's outburst and after you left, I spoke with Saffron. I'm really sorry Daisy, but the Thread Bare offer is off the table."

Daisy slumped down on the table, her face in her hands.

"Crap," she groaned. "I thought it would be. So not only did I get humiliated by not one, but two guys, and had my proposal shot down, but I also lost the buyer for my business. So, I am back at square one, with nothing to show for these ridiculous last few weeks!"

Daisy looked out to sea for a minute before turning back to Arabella and Royce.

"But you know, I think I may have realised something last night. All this time, I've been reacting to what's been happening, you know, the shop and Dan and Mack. I think I might have been expecting everyone else to make the decisions for me, or at least show me the way, so that I could sort my shit out. I really let all this drama get in the way of what really matters, and that is my career and the things I want to achieve in my life. This whole experience has been a wake-up call for me to get on with my life…and I almost failed at the first hurdle by getting sidetracked by two dumb guys. Even the Glass proposal was a bit misguided. I was still piggybacking off of two already successful people instead of going out there and making my own success."

Royce got up and walked around to his sister. He leant down and wrapped his arms around her in a tight hug.

"Hold up there with all that psychoanalysing. Actually, we have a bit of a surprise for you. Sit up straight, kid, and listen to what my amazing wife has to say." He kissed her cheek quickly before walking inside to refill the coffeepot.

Daisy sat up as Arabella passed over her laptop. "Have a read of this…"

Daisy looked at the screen. In Arabella's email account, there was an email from Ben and Stu.

It read:

Hi AB,

Sorry we didn't get to speak with you and Daisy last

night, but we were actually really excited to hear that Thread Bare has dropped out of the sale. We loved Daisy's proposal and we want to accept it, but with one small provision that we want to talk about more. Come and meet us for lunch at Vue at 1pm. We've booked a table on the veranda. Hope to see you all there!

S&B xx

Royce walked back out as Daisy looked up from the laptop, her eyes wide.

"What?" she exclaimed, "That is, I'm...umm..."

Arabella and Royce laughed affectionately as Daisy struggled to put her excitement into words.

"So, it seems like perhaps you were on the right track and were making your own success happen after all," Royce said with a smile.

"And there is nothing wrong with strategic partnerships when the partnership makes both sides stronger and better. Ben and Stu are no fools, they know what they want," added Arabella. "So, should I write back and say we'll be there?"

"Yes! Yes, bloody absolutely!"

"See, I told you to stick with me kid!" replied Arabella, reaching for the computer. "But seriously, what did you put in that proposal?"

———

Lunch was a hilarious affair. Stu and Ben were in fine form, and Sasha was much more relaxed away from the celebrity spotlight, proving to be just as entertaining as her dads. The group had taken over the front table on the veranda, and although the day was surly and cool, with winter well and truly on its way, the conversation was lively and warm. After the last few days, it felt good to laugh and relax.

"Daisy, as soon as we met you and heard you speak about the work you want to do with the artisans in Fiji, we knew there was a lot of synergy between our two business-es," explained Ben.

"We love your passion for designing and textiles," continued Stu. "And you obviously really love your shop, and we don't think you should give up on what you've worked so hard on. Your proposal couldn't have come at a better time! We really need someone to do a bit more of the research and travel part...this lot are keeping us pretty busy back in Noosa."

Stu looked across at his daughter, who was talking animatedly to Royce about her work experience as a marine biologist.

"Come work with us for a while...at the very least it will give you the chance to work with some old hands and learn the trade from a different perspective."

"Oh, there is just one thing. Arabella mentioned you were thinking about studying more. If you are interested, we'd love to make that part of the deal and we'd be thrilled to include tuition costs in the deal, if you were interested?"

"What do you say?" said Ben, elbowing Daisy in the ribs with a grin.

"You guys are amazing! Yes! I would love to!"

"It's such a good thing Mack contacted us," said Ben with a smile. "We would never have known you were the same Daisy that owned Garden and Bay if he hadn't called us the morning after the Fashion Festival launch party to tell us about the amazing young woman from Byron that we should look up."

"What are you talking about?" Daisy looked across the table. Royce and Arabella were looking away and Ben and Stu were smiling cheerfully.

"Where is that crazy kid this morning, anyway?" Stu asked, before Arabella kicked him swiftly in the shin. "And more importantly, did anyone ever find out who set off the sprinklers at the launch of Fashion Fest?" he continued with a grimace, getting the hint and rapidly changing the subject.

"I think we need to make a toast," said Arabella looking at her watch and hurriedly lifting her lime and soda.

"Yes!" exclaimed Stu, feeling completely lost and happy to steer the conversation back to something he understood. "Here's to our new extended family!"

They all raised their glasses in a toast, celebrating the beginnings of their new partnership.

Daisy smiled to herself as she watched Arabella rub her belly and wink lasciviously at her husband, who smiled back at her lovingly.

Yep, here's to family, she thought happily.

———

After making plans for Daisy to visit the factory in Noosa later in the week and review the contract, Daisy, Royce and Arabella said farewell to the Harrison-Mullers and walked down the creaky restaurant stairs to the street.

Royce looked at his watch. "We have one more thing to show you," he said secretively. "Come on."

Together they walked across Campbell Parade and down the sloping pathway towards the Pavilion. The day was still overcast, and the wind was cooler than it had been, which meant the beach was empty, save for a few lone fortune hunters waving their metal detectors over the soft sand.

Mack was waiting for them at the top of the stairs that led down to the beach.

"What is going on?" asked Daisy, looking at Arabella and Royce in confusion. "I don't want to see him. Mack, I don't want to see you. I never want to see you again."

Mack shoved his hands in his jacket pocket and nodded.

"Just listen to him, just for a bit," Royce said gently. "We'll be right up the hill." He put his arm around his wife and walked away to join a couple who were sitting at one of the picnic tables further up the grassy slope. There were no cameras this time, just Daisy and Mack, standing on the steps in front of the pavilion on a Monday afternoon, watching the wild, grey sea roiling before them.

"Can we sit?" asked Mack gently.

Daisy nodded, and they both took a seat on the cold concrete steps.

They sat there in silence for a while, until Mack turned to Daisy, his blue eyes searching hers for the smallest of encouragement. She sighed and turned to face him.

It was all the encouragement he needed. "This is the third time I've said this since last night and it doesn't get any easier," Mack said, his voice low and sad. "I've been taking drugs on and off for about fourteen years, ever since

Tess died. I was fifteen when it happened. And I think it was the only way I could cope at first. Shaun and I, we've been friends since primary school, but he was always the one who was getting into trouble and I always followed. He gave me my first joint, my first ecstasy pill, my first line of coke. And then it became a way of life and I started to embrace the whole wild child actor routine." Mack took a deep breath. "I'm an addict Daisy. Booze and drugs."

He paused for a moment to gather his thoughts and continued.

"I've been an unforgivable jerk to you, and to Arabella and Brian, and to my parents." He gestured up the hill to where Arabella and Royce were chatting quietly to the older couple.

"And most of all, I've been a jerk to myself. Tess would be really ashamed of me." Mack paused to wipe away a tear.

"I need you to know we didn't sleep together after the Ivy party. You were really high, and you were taking your clothes off, trying to seduce me. And I really wanted to sleep with you, Daisy. You are so beautiful and amazing, but you passed out, and I put you to bed. I didn't spike your drink either. That was Shaun. I am so angry that he did that, and I am so sorry. I was too high to know it at the time. Actually, I'm cutting myself off from Shaun. He's a terrible person and so many people have been telling me that for years. But I was also really angry at you because the journalist who wrote Dan's article sent me an advance copy, asking me if I wanted to comment. I was really hurt. I thought you were really starting to care about me and then I found out you had been sneaking over to his place, especially after we went to Store Beach. That's when I first realised I was falling for you. And when you told me about your accident, I thought you cared about me, too. I thought it meant you trusted me."

"I only went over once and it was really weird and nothing happened," Daisy interrupted. "It was going to fizzle out anyway, especially once I met you. Turns out he is a huge creep too," she finished with a small laugh.

Mack smiled sadly and nodded his head. "So now I am going to rehab. Before Hollywood, maybe even instead of Hollywood. Who knows? But the most important thing is that I kick this habit I've been dragging around for so long."

He paused and looked down at Daisy, his eyes clear and purposeful for the first time.

"And then I want to spend the rest of my life trying to make it up to you, if you will let me," he said.

Daisy, who was in tears now, started to speak, but Mack smiled and cut her off.

"Don't say anything yet. I'll chicken out if I stop talking. I am going to rehab for two months. And I can't see anyone or have any contact with anyone except my parents during that time. But Daisy Gardiner, I really think I am falling for you, for real, and I know I have no right to ask you this but I'm hoping that you might wait for me to get out of rehab and give me another chance to be a better man. When I get out, I am going to come here and sit on these steps and if you do care for me even the littlest, if you can forgive me for being the biggest creep, the most annoying, arrogant shit head that ever lived on this earth, I'd really like it if you were here to meet me."

Daisy reached over and took his hand. There was still a lot of damage to be undone, but for now it felt right for them to sit quietly, just holding hands and staring out to the sea.

Finally, Mack broke the silence.

"Hey, I, umm, I am really sorry about Garden and Bay. I heard that Thread Bare pulled out of the sale. I am so sorry for fucking that up for you," he said sadly. "I bought all the photos from the paper and made them take them all down, so that they couldn't keep publishing them. But I know it was too late."

Daisy smiled and wiped away her tears. "That was you? That was really nice. It was too late, but it was really nice. But actually, it turns out that was a blessing in disguise."

Daisy recounted the events of the day, then stopped. "Oh wait, before I forget, I need to give you back the money you paid me. You know I can't keep it now, right? Can I transfer it back to your account?"

"No, I don't want it."

"Come on Mack, please let me give it back to you…"

"No way, I mean it. You earned that money fair and square. I was such a jerk. I should give you more for having had to put up with me. Now tell me more about Ben and Stu."

As Daisy spoke about how Ben and Stu had accepted her proposal and had offered her the chance to finally go to university, as well as go into business with them, Mack looked down at Daisy's animated face and smiled tenderly.

"You know what, Tess would have really loved you. I just know it," he whispered, putting his arm around her and holding her tight.

Sixteen

———

Two months later, Daisy stood on the balcony of Royce and Arabella's apartment, pulling her coat and scarf tight, as the miserable July weather howled around her. Below her, the beach was empty. She still hadn't made up her mind if she was going to walk down and meet Mack.

The last two months had rushed by in a blur of contracts and planning and travel. Daisy had spent the first month in Noosa with Ben and Stu and the last two weeks in Fiji, visiting the team at Rise Above the Reef. She had just come back from an emotional trip home to Byron, where she had tearfully handed over the balance of money she owed her parents, plus a little extra to pay off the delayed mortgage payments.

"It's the least I can do," she had said firmly when Lola and Bill protested. "You are the best parents I could ask for. Thank you for standing by me all this time."

There was even enough left over to finally get her car fixed. For the first time that she could remember, Daisy felt in control of her own life and destiny. And she really liked it.

She thought back to the first morning she had stood on this balcony, not long after her first encounter with the world of celebrity. She remembered how small she felt and how terrified of change she had been.

Well, if nothing else, then these last few months have really taught me how to be brave and embrace the world, she thought to herself ruefully. She looked back inside at Royce and Arabella, who was now noticeably pregnant. They had just returned from their own trip to Fiji, a 'babymoon', more in love than ever and back to their usual selves.

True to his word, Mack had stayed silent throughout his time in rehab, focussing on getting better. His parents had been sending Daisy updates, and she was pleased to hear that he was doing well, charming the other patients and the doctors and nurses with his quick wit, sweet and kind now that the drugs were not holding him hostage.

Daisy was still not sure if she was going to go down and meet him. His parents, William and Linda, had told her she didn't have to go if she didn't feel up to it, that she shouldn't feel responsible for Mack's recovery. He had been awful to her, and they didn't blame her if she wanted to leave him in the past. Mack knew that as well and was prepared for her not to be there.

But somehow Daisy had ended up back in Bondi, on the very day that Mack had asked her to meet him. She didn't think that was a coincidence, despite her lingering uncertainty.

As she stood on the balcony, debating whether to go or stay, she spied a familiar figure, rugged up in a jacket and hoodie, standing on the top step of the stairs in front of the Pavilion.

It had to be him, she thought, her breath catching as she watched him looking around nervously.

Daisy stood frozen on the balcony. She had missed Mack so much over the last eight weeks. But he had also hurt her, and she wasn't sure she could trust him again. How could she know? Was he going to be different now that he was out of rehab?

As she looked down, she saw him turn and look up at the apartment, as if to say don't give up me just yet. It was all the sign she needed, and she turned automatically and ran out the door and down the stairs to the boardwalk. She didn't stop running until she reached the front of the Pavilion, praying he was still there.

When she reached the old concrete steps, she stopped to catch her breath, taking in the sight of the handsome tv star who had stolen her heart and broken it several times over, who was sitting in exactly the same spot where they'd said goodbye, eight long weeks before.

"Hello Mack," she called softly.

He stood up awkwardly, a hopeful expression spreading across his beautiful face. Daisy couldn't believe how calm he looked, how happy and healthy.

"Holy hell, it is so good to see you," she gasped, before throwing herself into his waiting arms.

"Hello Gardenia," he teased, holding her as tightly to him as he could, without breaking her. He laughed as she punched him lightly on the shoulder.

"You look so good," she said, pulling away to gaze at his face in adoration. "You look so calm and peaceful, like you are shining from the inside."

"I think that's because I am finally looking at you...you look amazing!" he said, a dopey smile plastered across his handsome face. "You look...stronger and happier. In control. Clearly, we have a lot to catch up on!"

"So, tell me everything!" Daisy exclaimed happily.

"First there are some things I need to say, ok?" he said, stepping back so he could hold Daisy's hands and look down into her sparkling green eyes. "Look at you. Look at your eyes. Do you know I dreamed about you every night in rehab? You were the only thing I thought about, not work, not the fame, just you and the hope that one day you might look at me again, the way that you did on top of the ferris wheel." Mack paused to tuck a strand of Daisy's hair behind one ear.

"Wait, that is not what I need to tell you though."

She stood, nervously wondering what he was going to say, holding his hands tightly.

"I have been standing here, an absolute wreck, wondering if you were going to show up." Mack continued uncertainly. "I wouldn't have blamed you if you didn't, but every part of me hoped you would. There is so much I have to say, Daisy, and so many amends to make. I can't believe I was so stupid and that maybe I lost you for good."

"But Daisy, even though you changed my world the second we met, I did terrible things to you, and I put you in danger. I need you to know that I am really, really sorry. Can you ever forgive me?"

Daisy's eyes filled with tears as she heard the sincerity in Mack's voice.

She nodded. "Of course I forgive you."

Mack smiled and sniffed tearfully as he continued. "I don't want to, and I hope it will never happen, but I might relapse and I might hurt you again and if I do, I am going to go back to rehab and start again. And you are under no obligation to stick around if that happens, you hear me? I have one chance to get this right with you and I don't want to keep hurting you. But I am going to work so hard to make sure it doesn't happen. But will you help me, will you remind me every day what it is I will lose if that happens?"

Daisy looked up at the beautiful man in front of her and nodded again. "Tell me what I can do Mack," she said, smiling now.

"Just say you love me Daisy, as much as I love you,"

"I love you, Mack. Of course I love you!"

"Then there is only more thing I need to do," he said with a grin.

"What's that?" asked Daisy.

Mack's heart beat faster and faster as he bent his head and finally kissed her, gently at first, and tenderly, but harder and deeper, as she responded, wrapping her arms tightly around his neck, while he scooped her into him and held her close. Not counting those lost hours at the Ivy, they had only kissed like this a handful of times. But for both of them, it felt like finally coming home. They kissed for what seemed like hours more, making up for the months in rehab, and making up for all the hurt and pain they had caused each other over the last few tumultuous months.

"So what happens now?" asked Daisy, when they had come up for air and sat wrapped up in each other's arms on the steps.

"Well, I don't know about you, but there is something I've been waiting a really long time to do," Mack said, nuzzling her neck suggestively.

Daisy smiled and blushed, barely able to believe the handsome Mack Boddington was really hers. "Hmm, yes, well, that is pretty urgent," she teased. "But after that, what do we do? I mean, where are you going to live? How are we going to make this work?"

"Well, I definitely lost the Michael Bay contract. And Home and Away won't take me back. I don't blame them. I was a bloody train wreck. But lucky for me, the Wes Anderson film is going ahead—unluckily for them, one of the leads broke their leg and so production has been put on hold for six months. If I can stay clean and sober for that time, the part is still mine. And then I'll be in LA for nine months for the shoot."

"So, do you think you can stay sober for the whole time?"

"I really do. I know it's only been two months so far. I messed up so badly, but somehow, I have this second chance.

A second chance with work and a second chance with you. I don't want to mess any of it up again. But that means I have four months before I need to be in LA." Mack looked down at Daisy. "And I think I should probably get out of Sydney, you know, get out of the bubble. What about you? Where are you living now? How were your last eight weeks?"

"My last eight weeks were both amazing and agonising," laughed Daisy, filling him in on her time in Noosa and Fiji, and more recently, back in Byron.

"Although I was still so mad at you, all I wanted to do was call you up and tell you everything that's been going on. It's been amazing, and I am so excited to finally tell you."

Daisy looked up at Mack shyly. "I know you didn't want me to give you the money back. So I donated it to CMRI instead. I hope that's ok?"

Mack smiled and nodded, clearly touched by her gesture. "Holy heck Gardenia, I always knew you were destined for big and wonderful things from the first moment I saw you," he teased.

"You dumb ass, that is such a lie. You were such a jerk to me!"

"I was such a jerk. But you changed my life completely, you know, that day we met at the Lost at Sea party. From the moment you held out your hand, I was a goner!"

Daisy's heart flip-flopped as she remembered the time she had first met Mack and how she had been unable to breathe standing next to the gorgeous actor.

What a difference a few months can make, she marvelled, as she squeezed his hand tightly.

"You know, I have to go back to Byron for a few weeks, to spend some time at the shop, now that it is being incorporated into the Glass label." Daisy looked up at Mack thoughtfully. "Why don't come back with me? I think we could keep you out of trouble up there. My mum will cook endless amounts of food for you, and Dad and Jeff, that's Arabella's dad, will take you surfing every day and keep you healthy. And my parent's house is a huge old farmhouse, so there is plenty of space. They will love you. Once they get over being mad at you. I just don't want to be away from you until we figure out how we are going to make this work."

"As long as we stick together, we will always make this work," replied Mack, kissing the top of Daisy's head. "But I'd love to come with you. There is just one thing we need to do before we go."

"I already told you that's first on the agenda!" replied Daisy with a cheeky grin.

"Haha, dork, after that!" They looked out over the cold, wintery Pacific as it crashed in the grey twilight. "Will you come and have dinner with my parents?" he asked with a smile. "They really want to meet you."

"I'd love to," replied Daisy happily, snuggling deeper into Mack's warm arms.

Up above them, the bars at the Pavilion had turned on their multi-coloured lanterns and Bondi's beautiful were gathering, desperate to be seen in all the right places, despite the murky weather. The sounds of a Katy Perry song floated out over the cold evening, an unofficial anthem for the cult of the Sydney celebrity...

Are we crazy?
Living our lives through a lens,
Trapped in a white picket fence, like ornaments,
So comfortable we're living in a bubble,
So comfortable we cannot see the trouble,
So put your rose-coloured glasses on and party on.

For more information on the not-for-profit organisations
mentioned in the book, please go to:
Rise Beyond the Reef www.risebeyondthereef.org
Children's Medical Research Institute - Jeans for Genes
www.cmrijeansforgenes.org.au

Primrose Series

By Tanya Renee

Prairie Sky

Prairie Nights

Prairie Fire

A New Page

by Aimee MacRae

It Happened in Paris

By Michelle Beesley

Mim and Wiggy's Grand Adventure

By Jay McKenzie

For more information visit:

www.serenadepublishing.com

About the Author

Megan Krolik grew up on the beaches and in the sugarcane fields of Queensland, Australia, cementing early on a love for all things hot and tropical. Megan has since spent many years working as a humanitarian aid worker on remote islands in the Pacific and deep in the jungles of Asia, these beautiful and intriguing places inspiring many of Megan's fictional adventures.

Megan has written three novels, as well as a non-fiction coffee-table book for the Women Inspired: Sunshine Coast project. In 2021 she won a place in the Queensland Writer's Centre Scriptable program with her television screenplay She won the Pineapple, and she has written and directed two plays with BATS Theatre Company Inc.

Megan has two master's degrees in international development and emergency management and has published several journal articles, field guides and policy papers. She currently works for the world's largest humanitarian network by day and writes funny love stories by night.

Acknowledgments

My grandmother Beryl gave me a typewriter when I was about eight years old and patiently listened as I bashed out A Country Practice fan fiction and then read it out loud to her. While the writing team at ACP was safe, it was a defining moment for me, and I've been writing ever since. Beryl would have been so proud...but definitely a little scandalized by Mack's adventures. Not sure I would have read it to her this time!

To Jaya, Sarah and Celeste, thanks for growing up and growing old with me. I love you and can't imagine my life any other way.

To Melissa Elk, the next big thing in children's literature and Evangeline Cachinero, Melbourne's best digital and textile artist, it's been a long creative journey since our uni days, and I am so grateful we've been doing this together for so long! I can't wait to see what you both do next.

To Gaby, thank you for entertaining me with all your behind-the-scenes stories of life in the Sydney celebrity bubble. I told you all those nights eating Thai takeaway on the floor of our Bondi flat watching Hart of Dixie would amount to something! And to Hilda and Jo, thanks for all of the many adventures in our very own Sydney bubble.

To Bernadette and Jemma, and Jemma's elephants at

the Elephant Valley Project, thank you for letting me write part of this book in your lovely homes/jungles in Cambodia.

Thank you to the amazing Allison, Seema and Sally for all the reads and feedback. All the good bits are directly because of you!

Thank you to Fanni and Leeanne for being my wonderful social media cinematographers. Dancing around Budapest in a ball gown with you both will be some of my favourite memories of all time!

To my incredible friends and colleagues at the IFRC ROE office in Budapest and the ARC office in Australia. Thank you for letting me occasionally distract you from the important and life-changing work you do, with all my not so serious stories of books and plays and book launch parties. It's an honour to work alongside you all.

And finally, to Sarah at Serenade Publishing, thank you for taking a chance on me and giving me the opportunity to make this long held dream come true!